MARY JANE

*Big Zwack!
Treasure Your History!
Anne Marie Fritz*

MARY JANE

A TRUE AMERICAN TALE

ANNE MARIE FRITZ

TATE PUBLISHING
AND ENTERPRISES, LLC

Mary Jane
Copyright © 2014 by Anne Marie Fritz. All rights reserved.

No part of this publication may be reproduced, stored in a retrieval system or transmitted in any way by any means, electronic, mechanical, photocopy, recording or otherwise without the prior permission of the author except as provided by USA copyright law.

This novel is a work of fiction. Names, descriptions, entities, and incidents included in the story are products of the author's imagination. Any resemblance to actual persons, events, and entities is entirely coincidental.

The opinions expressed by the author are not necessarily those of Tate Publishing, LLC.

Published by Tate Publishing & Enterprises, LLC
127 E. Trade Center Terrace | Mustang, Oklahoma 73064 USA
1.888.361.9473 | www.tatepublishing.com

Tate Publishing is committed to excellence in the publishing industry. The company reflects the philosophy established by the founders, based on Psalm 68:11,
"The Lord gave the word and great was the company of those who published it."

Book design copyright © 2014 by Tate Publishing, LLC. All rights reserved.
Cover design by Nikolai Purpura
Interior design by Jimmy Sevilleno

Published in the United States of America

ISBN: 978-1-63122-655-7
1. Fiction / Historical
2. Fiction / War & Military
14.02.24

For Jon, thank you for always believing I could and should do this.

For Taylor and Hayden, always my inspiration. So you will know where you came from and how incredibly strong you can be.

For my aunt Mary Jane and uncle Bob, the keepers of the family history. Thank you for sharing so much of yourself with us.

Introduction

FOR THE CHIPPEWA people, without their generosity and love, my family line would not have survived.

As Americans, our history is a unique story. Unless you are of native descent, your ancestors traveled great distances, through great peril and adversity, to come to a new world for what they hoped was a better life for themselves and their children. Today, we are the recipients of this tenacious bravery. Our nation's history is riddled with greed, aggression, and hate. But intertwined with this are stories of love, compassion, and understanding. This is one of those tales.

My family emigrated from Sweden like thousands of others, looking for a better life. A life of freedom and opportunity. My family would not have survived their journey had it not been for Native people.

For this, I am eternally grateful.

Anne Marie Fritz

I wrote this story to immortalize a chapter of our history for my own children. So they too would remember the tales passed down from one generation to the next. I wrote these words so we would all remember and rejoice in the strength of the human heart. So we would not forget the power of the human spirit and its impact on our culture today.

The Family Line

Hans Greves Nilsson (Nelson)—Bertha Parson Nilsson (Nelson)

1. Mary Jane
2. Annie Janet (Nettie)
3. Eric
4. Alfred
5. Henry
6. Christine Hattie
7. George
8. Isaar
9. Charlie
10. Baby boy Jonathon (actual name is unknown)
11. Baby boy Hans (actual name is unknown)

Anne Marie Fritz

Mary Jane Nilsson—John Wilhelm Anderson
1. Vivian Louise
2. Sierra Clara
3. George Walter
4. Aleck "Al" John
5. Mary Fredricka
6. Mabel Bertha

Mabel Bertha Anderson—Perrine Eglin
1. Mary Jane Eglin Steiner
2. Jack Willits Eglin

Jack Eglin—Darlene Stephens
1. Anne Marie Eglin Fritz (author)
2. Matthew Aleck Eglin

❖ Mary Jane ❖

On the Mountain of the Prairie,
On the great Red Pipe-Stone Quarry,
Gitche Manito, the mighty,
He the Master of Life, descending,
On the red crags of the quarry
Stood erect, and called the nations,
Called the tribes of men together.

—Henry Wadsworth Longfellow
"The Song of Hiawatha"

The Beginning

THE RED ROCK Quarry had called to men for thousands of years.

Since the beginning of time.

Here they used sticks or stones to chip away the soft clay that smothered the treasured stone beneath. Pink limestone was commonly found in the surrounding area, but it was the rich blood-red catlinite stone that sung to the hearts and minds of these early Americans.

Pipestone.

When the world was fresh and new, the great creator Wakan Tanka was disappointed with his human children. They displayed greed and anger and did not take care of the creators gifts. Wakan Tanka called out to the great water monster, Unktehi.

"Wash away the unworthy" was the command.

Unktehi caused the waters to rise and the currents to swirl until the water had encompassed all of the land.

The creator allowed only one small section of earth to remain, a small hill. Too small for everyone to find sanctuary. The humans climbed up this hill, carrying the wounded and weak. But it was no use. The rocks tumbled down, crushing any in their path.

"Is there not a single human that is worthy?" cried Wakan Tanka.

Wanblee Galeshka, the great eagle, hearing the creator's cry, flew over the small rocky crag that emerged from the black torrent of angry water. His insightful eyes located a young girl, clinging to the slippery stones, her feet washed out from under her. She raised her small face to the angry sun and silently spoke to the heavens. The eagle, Wanblee, flew over her repeatedly, intently listening to the heart of the small girl. With talons sharp and strong, he dove down toward the child.

Seeing the great eagle descend, the child let go of her hold and raised her arms to the bird. Wanblee Galeshka grasped her smooth young flesh with the tenderness of a loving parent. He flew her to safety, to the tallest peak of the rocky island.

"This child is worthy," he cried up to the creator. "She prayed you take her and let the others survive."

The waters immediately drained away from the soil. The rock crag was stained red from the blood of the dead. A constant reminder to the People how precious the gift of life is and how easily it can be taken away.

This red rock was for ever more sacred. The creator made the red stone easy to carve. And so, for thousands of years, Indians will do pilgrimage to the Red Rock Quarry. They will dig and carve and polish the sacred stone into ceremonial pipes. Pipes of peace. Pipes of praise.

They will use the stone pipes to teach their history to generations to come and to tell the story of how the human life was spared because of one small voice of love and charity. And for thousands of years, they will strive to live a life worthy of this great sacrifice.

Meeting of Men
Minnesota
Territory 1858

THE RED ROCK Quarry was a land of history and peace. It was sacred ground for all of the People, no matter what their tribe. It was the perfect location for the meeting. Chief Wabasha of the Santee Sioux wished to meet with other Sioux leaders. It took Wabasha many meetings around the sacred fire throughout the winter to convince his fellow warriors that in order for the Sioux to survive, there must be peace with their Indian enemy, the Chippewa. It took Wabasha another full moon to convince his warriors that they needed to meet with the leaders of the Chippewa tribe from the north.

This was an important meeting but uncomfortable, to say the least. Historically, the Sioux and the Chippewa were mortal enemies. Years of conflicts over hunting grounds around the lakes of Minnesota territory had bred nothing but hatred between them. Generation after generation knew nothing but loathing and fear when the other name was spoken. So much blood had been shed—too much blood. Perhaps too much to be forgotten, even momentarily.

Even the name Sioux itself is proof of this legacy. Sioux is a French corruption of the Chippewa word for enemy. Meeting at the Red Rock Quarry was the only neutral territory that would be honored by all invited.

"What makes you think these dirty pigs will even come tonight?" Little Crow sneered.

Little Crow was a powerful man in the Santee Sioux tribe. He would be a chief someday soon. Wabasha knew Little Crow wanted war, war against the Chippewa and war against the whites. That was the cause for the concern that clouded his eyes.

"They will come," Chief Wabasha muttered at he stood.

"They have to come," he said more to himself than the crowd now gathering around the fire.

Within the great teepee, there were now almost twenty men and more ducking into the warmth of the dwelling every minute. All Sioux—brave, strong, trustworthy. They sat on the comfort of layers of thick, lush buffalo robes that had been scattered around the fire pit. The talk continued to grow louder as each one shared a view point similar to Little Crows.

Maybe the Chippewa would not come. Perhaps this did not concern the Chippewa people as much as it did the Sioux.

All the Sioux tribes had a representative. It was a distinguished group of leaders to be sure. Wabasha looked proudly around the sacred fired at the faces he admired. These were men he had fought next to in battle before. These were men who he knew would help him defend his family and loved ones. These were men, Wabasha himself was prepared to die defending.

The Teton Sioux, also known as the Lakota Sioux, had three chiefs here to speak and hopefully listen as well. They had come the farthest, from the great mountain range to the west. The Lakota were known as great hunters and warriors. Wabasha silently prayed that they would be open to a peaceful conclusion to their people's dilemma.

The Dakota, Nakota, and Yankto Sioux came from the Black Hills territory. The sacred homeland of the Sioux people, where the first Sioux came into existence thanks to the Great Creator. They were also known for their hunting skills but lived in an area where they traded with and lived in close proximity to several other tribes. Perhaps they will be open to peace, at least open to discussing how to obtain a peaceful relationship with other red men. These warriors would most likely understand that the Sioux could not fight off enemy tribes as well as whites simultaneously and survive.

And finally, the Santee Sioux from the Minnesota territory. His own family. Glancing over his shoulder, Chief Wabasha looked at the men around the fire. The men he respected and loved. They were his brothers, his sons, his friends. How many of them will be here to sit around another fire in ten winters if peace is not agreed upon tonight?

Wabasha was shaken from his wandering thoughts when a strong arm grabbed his shoulder.

"The Chippewa are here," spat the Sioux warrior guarding the entrance to the teepee.

Ojibwa was the name preferred by their enemies to the north. So, of course, it was Chippewa in which the majority of the Sioux people will continue to call them. The word *Chippewa* in actuality meant *puckered*. Most likely, it was spoken first by a French trapper in connection with the style of moccasins produced by these Indians. The gathering across the top of the foot made the moccasins fit well and quite comfortably. However, to the Sioux warriors, it symbolized the faces of their enemy on the battlefield and was used as a reminder of the Sioux superiority.

The talking around the fire immediately ceased. The silence was deafening and ominous. As several men began to rise, Wabasha silently pushed his open palm to the earth, signaling he wished them to stay seated as their *guests* arrived. They did as they were asked. Wabasha was well respected throughout the Sioux tribe. He had a reputation of being a fiercely strong warrior; this earned him glory. But it was his quiet brilliance and ability to communicate with red men and white alike to better the lives of his people—all his people—that earned him the respect he witnessed this night.

Wabasha stepped back and straightened his back, bringing himself to his full height as the first Chippewa Chief bent to enter the teepee.

Wabasha extended his right hand. It was grasped by his guest. The men held on to each others forearms hand to elbow as their dark eyes locked. Each searching the other mans stare, trying to read his thoughts.

"Hau, Dakota." Wabasha firmly said as he shook the man's arm. *Hello, friend.*

"Hau." *Hello.* His voice was low but strong. Knowing that all eyes were upon him, he returned the arm shake and looked his host again directly in the eye. Great concern was mirrored there.

The Chippewa chief's words flooded the silent teepee. "It is good we are here. We have much to discuss, your people and mine. The Great Creator will be pleased to see us here tonight."

The Chippewa chief was called *Baswenaazhi.* Crane. It was fitting. He stood a full head and shoulder taller than Wabasha. His hair was long and thick and dominated with gray strands that were pulled back and tied with a small piece of animal hide at the base of his neck. A necklace of grizzly bear claws circled his broad neck and shoulders. Bells and beads sang out from his decorated, puckered moccasins as he moved counter-clockwise around the fire to take his seat.

Following the old tradition of moving throughout the teepee paying reverence to the creator impressed the men already present. Perhaps these Chippewas were not heathens after all. Chief Crane was joined by two more men, both as tall as their chief, but much younger. One was his son, *Doodem*, Thunderbird. And the third was a young medicine man called *Nooka*, Tender Bear. All three men where dressed in light buckskins and loin cloths made of tanned elk hides. They wore cotton shirts, metal jewelry, and brightly colored beads hinting at the strong trade relations their people had with the Canadian French and British alike.

A strong family resemblance was obvious with these three men. Their height, broad stance, piercing eyes, sharp nose, square jaws, and high cheek bones allowed one to easily see they were closely related. The obvious difference was the red handprint painted across the mouth of their holy man, medicine man, the one called *Nooka*, Tender Bear. The two followed the lead of their chief as they entered the dwelling and took their offered seat around the fire.

With the men all now sitting around the sacred fire, Wabasha was ready to begin.

May the spirits be on his side tonight.

The smoke curled lazily up toward the gaping mouth of the teepee. Sage was placed in the fire, following traditions, giving thanks to the creator. The heavy aroma hung on the fabric of the dwelling and each man. The attending closed their eyes and deeply inhaled the scented air around them, each lost in their own quiet prayer for a moment.

A large red pipe was then packed with tobacco. Wabasha tossed some of the tobacco into the fire atop the sage. A plum of heavily scented smoke curled toward the smoke hole and disappeared into the night sky above.

"For the Creator," he said.

The pipe was well crafted from the sacred stone that they now sat upon. It was decorated with eagle feathers to honor the great bird that saved all of mankind. The pipe was passed first to Chief Crane who drank deeply from it. He slowly blew the blue smoke into the fire.

His deep voice followed the path of the smoke. "For the spirits of our ancestors."

He then passed the pipe around the fire. Person to person. Slowly, each man inhaled from the sacred pipe, then exhaled, and washed his face and head with the sacred smoke. Finally, when the pipe was returned to Wabasha, it was time to begin discussing why they were all there.

The Great White Chief in Washington, DC, wants to purchase the Minnesota territory. They again want the People to move away from their homelands, to leave their holy grounds, to abandoned the bones of their dead. The Chippewa or Ojibwas tribe was huge. The third largest tribe in North America. Their lands surrounded the Great Lakes and spread into what was called Canada. The Sioux was big and strong and not afraid to defend their territory. But were they large enough to stand up to the whites without an alliance between the two tribes? And could an alliance between these two tribes be trusted for an extended period of time?

Since the War of 1812, when the Chippewa had joined forces with the British and fought against the Americans and the Great White Chief James Madison, they had one thing the Sioux did not have enough of—guns. The Chippewa had used those British guns on the Sioux, and it was a bloodbath that none of them wanted to remember this night.

The discussion went on into the early morning hours. Tempers flared regularly, but the two chiefs masterfully put out each fire with their calm and powerful words. It was obvious that they could not obtain a trusted partnership. But a temporary peace was definitely a possibility.

"The Ojibwa will never again sign the White Man's papers," stated Chief Crane.

"A treaty, they call it. The whites have no honor. They follow no law but their own, and they break it whenever it pleases them. They fear the British, and the British are friends of the Ojibwa. We will stay north, around the great waters. We will not sell our Mother Earth. But you have my word, we will not make war on the Sioux." With that said, Chief Crane reached for the pipe. He loaded and lit it himself. After drawing from the sacred pipe, he handed it directly to Wabasha.

A promise was made.

The Sioux would be on their own. But peace with their neighbors had been promised. The Sioux would sell their land to the white chief. It was the only way to ensure peace with Washington, DC. They would move west and join the other Sioux Bands. This was not the ideal situation, but at least, no more blood would be spilled on this ground. Wabasha breathed a sigh of relief as he watched the pipe circle the fire. Once again, the power of the Red Rock Quarry protected the future of the People. Once again, the future was in their hands.

The Land of Plenty
Sweden 1858

THEY WERE LATE. The church was already full. Full of neighbors eager to hear what the pastor had discovered. For months, maybe even years, the locals of Orsa, Sweden, had dreamed of moving to America. Tonight may be the night that those dreams finally came to pass.

Dozens of horses patiently stood tethered, still hooked up to their wagons, carriages, or other burdens. Their owners too excited or perhaps too distracted to give their comfort another thought.

Storm clouds gathered above the slopping hills and the sea pounded on the rocks below. The turbulent weather was, however, also forgotten or overlooked. The anxiety and excitement was palatable as the Nilsson family walked into the back of the little white building that served as the school house and church for the 204 residence of this small Swedish village.

"Standing room only," Hans Nilsson whispered to his oldest child, Mary Jane. "Find Mama a seat, would you?" Hans juggled a sleeping five-year-old boy from one hip to the other. Isaar was really too big to be carried, but his father did not want to leave him outside in the wagon. Today they would witness history. History that would affect them all. Even the sleeping giant in his arms.

Mary Jane meandered through the crowd, apologizing and offering salutations as she did. She raised her hand above her head when a vacant seat was discovered for her mother to sit. Bertha Nilsson was a beautiful woman. Her wavy, raven-black hair and deep green eyes often awarded her another glance, even from those who were accustomed to her rare beauty. She appeared to glow even more radiant as she followed her daughter's wave with her newborn son wrapped snuggly in her arms. Jonathon was her tenth child. This, of course, made her husband Hans very proud, but secretly, Bertha prayed it would be her last.

As Bertha found her seat, several turned toward her to coo at the baby.

"What a lovely child. He has your eyes already."

"Sweet little Jonathon. Look at him sleep."

"Perhaps he will spend his first birthday in America." What a thought, could that be possible?

It was not a difficult decision for a Swede to immigrate to America. Thousands of Swedish immigrants had already braved the voyage across the Atlantic Ocean to the Land of Plenty. Just forty years earlier, the economic disaster began that still had an enormous impact on the Swedish population. Gustav IV was known as the weak and incompetent king of Sweden. Years of very costly and unsuccessful wars with Russia and later the French left the coffers depleted. This was coupled with widespread crop failure that left thousands starving throughout the Swedish countryside, with little or no attention from their king. Conspirators surrounded Gustav. They persuaded the crown with threats of imprisonment and even assassination, to abdicate his throne. But it was too late for the poor and hungry. As the king stepped down, they found no salvation. Today, an irresponsible and erratic leader was no longer the concern, but rebuilding the strength of this shattered country was. It was a slow and tedious process.

The American Revolution had set the standards for underprivileged people everywhere. Since that amazing moment in 1776, people every where claimed their patriotism. And in doing so, they demanded freedoms like America. A constitution like America's. Sweden's constitution allowed for the first time, freedom of the press.

Newspapers and flyers could be found in every home in Sweden, exclaiming that America was the land of hope for the common people. Over and over, the newspapers stressed that the United States was the land of plenty.

"The home of everything that was promising for the world's downtrodden."

Sweden's first novelist, Fredrika Bremer, wrote a compelling and very popular book after her visit to American shores. This provided the first close-up view of America and what opportunities lay within her splendors. And who after all was down trodden if not the Swedish population burdened with the task of cleaning up the mess left behind by such a sloppy and selfish king?

"What a glorious new Scandinavia might not Minnesota become!" Bremer rallied.

This was the spark that ignited the flame that burned with in the walls of the church this night. Hans Nilsson, his family, friends, and neighbors all held their breath as they waited for their pastor to speak.

Pastor Vance Dominic rose. He took a step to the altar and raised his hands above his head, palms open to his congregation. This was done out of habit, more than anything, for the crowd was silent with the exception of a few children whimpering as they buried their tired faces into their mother's bosom or lap, complaining that they had already been to church this week.

"Thank you for coming tonight on such short notice," he began. Pastor Dom, as the children called him, tried to calm his nerves. But his voice gave way to his excitement at the news he was about to share with the men and women that had been his friends and neighbors for the past many years. Looking out into their eager faces, he had flashes of their lives and how they had intertwined together over the years. He had married Janet and Charles Olmstead. He had just buried Mrs. Sheldon's husband last fall, and he had baptized all ten of the Nilsson children, including baby Jonathon just last month. He loved these people, and he silently prayed they would be as thrilled as he was.

Pastor Dom cleared his throat. Again, he tried to calm his nerves. He wanted these people to agree because it was what they wanted, not because their pastor had suggested it. It would require an enormous sacrifice from each and every one of them.

"I have heard back from our friends in America. Minnesota territory is vying for statehood. They, however, need to increase their citizenship, their voters, so that statehood will be approved by the United States Congress," he said as he clasped his hands excitedly together. He paused for dramatic effect or to catch his wind. He was not sure.

"What does that have to do with us?" asked a member from the crowd.

"Everything!" Pastor Dom replied. "In order to have a vote, to be a citizen, we must live in the Minnesota territory." Again, the pastor paused. His audience was not responding to this news as he had hoped. The silence quickly became awkward.

"Father Dom?" It was Hans Nilsson. Thank God. A voice of reason. Maybe Hans could assist.

"Yes, Hans."

"So any news about the land, our land, in Minnesota?"

"Oh yes!" he said, steadier this time. "I apologize. It is just so thrilling! Congress wants Minnesota to be a slave free state. So if there's enough citizens, landowners will vote for this territory to be free soil, and statehood will be granted. They do not wish another bleeding Kansas on their hands. So to make this happen…"

A lot of blood had been shed on Kansas soil due to conflicts from its citizens over this very topic. The controversial issue with Kansas's statehood had put up a temporary blockade on other states west of the Mississippi River wanting to join the union. With war looming, the Congress was eager to approve statehood to any territory willing to swear an allegiance to the north and of course remain slave free. Minnesota was next in line.

Pastor Dom took a deep breath and again spread his arms out over the heads of his audience. "To make this happen," he repeated, "they are selling land within our price range if we promise to honor our pledge of remaining loyal to Washington, DC."

It took the crowd a moment to process the information. They were again quiet. Too quiet, Pastor Dom found this tremendously unnerving. Again, thankfully, Hans Nilsson raised his hand to be heard.

"So we will be allowed to purchase this land in Minnesota territory for the small amount we offered. And all we have to do, to become an American citizen and land owner today, is to vote? Vote to be loyal to the Union?"

Many people in this room had never had the right to vote before. Many did not understand the power that a single vote could hold. But Hans did. Hans understood all to well. He remembered not having a say; not having a say about how his own land was utilized.

Pastor Dom nodded his head like a puppet on a string. Finally, he could see the glint of excitement in the eyes looking upon him. Finally, he could feel the wave of excitement ripple through the room.

"Yes, and we must vote to be slave free," he said, clapping his hands together again. That would not be a difficult task, as a whole the Swedish population had been eternally against slavery since the beginning of time.

"Well," Hans began as he glanced over the heads toward his beautiful wife. She smiled and nodded her head. That was all the encouragement he needed.

"Where's my ballot?"

Statehood

O N MAY 11, 1858, Minnesota became the thirty-second state to join the Union. Minnesota was immediately known as the Land of 10,000 Lakes, The Star of the North, and even The Empire State. All could be claimed as factual descriptions of America's newest addition, but in actuality, what had Washington, DC, smiling was that they now had a state loyal to the Union that controlled the head waters of the great Mississippi River. This made Minnesota a strategic location for commercial manufacturing. With manufacturing came workers, and workers were, of course, taxpayers. This meant money—money to support the Union cause. And men in Washington D.C., were tallying it up.

The winter of 1858 was uncommonly brutal. Temperatures dipped well below zero for weeks at a time. The ten thousand lakes that had made Minnesota so appealing froze over freezing travel, trade, and commerce as well. The capital's desire to "fill Minnesota with

American citizens" was slow in coming. But of course, there was the promise of new immigrants that would be arriving in the spring. There was always spring.

The winter was not only devastating to Congress and the National Bank, but it was extremely harsh on settlers as well. White and red. The people who had called this territory home for centuries were hit hard. The Santee Sioux had agreed to sell twenty-four million acres to the federal government. The $1,410,000 promised in the treaty, however, did not come. It was now doubtful that it ever would.

Chief Wabasha had moved his people west of the Red Rock Quarry like he promised he would. His people were now freezing and hungry. Trapped by the winter storms and not in their normal hunting grounds, food was scarce. Purchasing supplies was out of the question since the federal funds had still not been received. Wabasha had no choice. A meeting of the People was called by Little Crow, who was now Chief Little Crow, after a very successful raid on the Black Feet last summer.

The long house was sturdily built with logs and sealed with pitch. Grass mats and buffalo robes carpeted the dirt floor, and several fire pits were ablaze in the center of the dwelling. Bed bunks were elevated off of the frozen earth and lined each wall. One door made of wood and hide, faced east, to greet the morning sun each new day. Women and children had been chased out of the long house minutes before the prominent men in the tribe began to enter. One by one, warriors, chiefs, and medicine men arrived. All were quiet and reverent.

Traditions were followed. Elders sat closest to the fire, the peace pipe was passed, the chiefs spoke first, and then every other member was heard. One powerful and passionate voice at a time.

"We must travel east to the great water. There we will find game," Little Crow began.

"We promised the White Chiefs we would not travel near the great water. The great water, the great lakes are now the lands of the whites and the Chippewa," Wabasha replied.

"Why should we keep our word to the white man when he can not keep his to us?" responded Little Crow in a fierce voice just short of a growl.

"The white man's word means nothing!" spat another.

"You cannot trust a man who puts different words on paper, then speaks another from his lips," said another.

"You cannot trust men who think they can own Mother Earth," said yet another.

The voices grew loud in agitation. Wabasha pushed his hand toward the blaze, a signal that he wished to speak. All fell silent.

"I have heard you all, and you speak the truth. We have reason to distrust the white man. Many reasons. General Pope promised much money if we moved our people west. We did. Now our people are in a new land, and they are cold, and they are hungry, and where is the money and supplies promised? Our food supplies are running low, and hunting is difficult here in this valley. Perhaps the creator is angry with us for selling Mother

Earth to the Great White Chief. I do not know." He paused when a voice interrupted him.

It was Little Crow.

"General Pope does not care about our children. The white man does not care about his promise. We must raid. We must feed our people. And we must do it now."

Wabasha could tell by the nodding of many heads around the fire that Little Crow spoke what many had wanted to say and wanted to hear. The peace was over; war was drawing near.

General John Pope was in charge of the Minnesota Indian Affairs. Within one year, the amount of power Pope would wield would shake the nation to its foundation. Abraham Lincoln was elected in a landslide as America's sixteenth president. Endorsed by Lincoln, John Pope will ride that wave to his own greedy and bloody success.

John Pope was the eldest son of Federal Judge Nathaniel Pope. Nathaniel was a well-respected, prominent, and extremely powerful voice in Washington. He was also a dear friend to the once attorney-at-law, Abraham Lincoln. It was at the summer cotillion at the Pope home that young Abraham Lincoln would be introduced to their beloved cousin, Mary Todd. Just a few years later, John Pope himself will oversee the marriage of Mary Todd to the ambitious Lincoln. These connections offered many opportunities for the young and determined John Pope. As a graduate of the United States Military Academy, it seemed his future laid in front of young John like a garden path. All he had to do was select which path he wished to take. Indian affairs offered Pope control, power and a bloody battle now and again. The latter being the honey for this aggressive bee.

With Lincoln in the White House, tensions in the south rose like the evening tide. South Carolina will be the first state to secede from the nation, and within a few short months of six, other Southern states will follow suit. The line was drawn. Southern states swore an allegiance to a new nation, The Confederate States of America, and elected their own president. President Jefferson Davis.

With a Civil War looming, money was of grave concern. By 1861, the federal government still had not paid any money to the Santee Sioux Indians for their section of southern Minnesota. Yet hundreds of thousands of white immigrants poured into the New Scandinavia, looking for an opportunity to make a better life for themselves and their families, staking claims on this Indian land.

Chief Little Crow had become a prominent voice with in his tribe. He was young, strong, intense, and determined to make the whites pay for months and months of hunger and death. This night, he would have revenge.

A small raiding party of twenty men prepared to cross the invisible boundary. They were looking for food and blankets as much as they could carry. Their target was a settlement that sat along the river near the twin cities, Minneapolis and St. Paul. Little Crow painted his horse with blue and yellow lines. They resembled lightening bolts diving toward the earth as they snaked down the horse's legs. Matching bolts of energy adorned Little Crows high cheek bones. With his jet-black hair pulled back in two braids that hung down his bare back to his waist, he appeared fierce and strong. A power to be reckoned with.

In one smooth motion, Little Crow buried his hands in his painted steed's mane and swung his agile body atop. A feathered spear was handed to him as well as the only rifle that he owned. He carried a knife on his thick thigh and another at his waist. Little Crow looked around him, at the people of his tribe, the people he loved and cherished. He was doing this for them. They needed supplies, and if he could satisfy his ravenous hunger for revenge at the same time, it was all the better.

He thrust his right arm, clutching the spear into the air. His war cry pierced the night sky with the promise of what was to come. His party responded with energy that pleased him. Searching the crowd, Little Crow finally met the face he was seeking. Wabasha nodded his head, offering a silent wish for success. Little Crow returned the nod but could not help but recognize the sadness that engulfed the elder chief's eyes.

Immigration West 1862

THE ONLY WAY to America from Sweden was obviously by ship. Mary Jane had never been on a ship and had mixed feelings about the voyage. She was filled with excitement at the prospect of something new and adventurous while anxious and nervous of leaving everything familiar to her behind. The prospect of immigrating to a whole new world was no doubt intimidating, but thousands of people will go, all looking for a better life for themselves and their family.

The *Norske Love* was the name of their ship. This type of ship was also known as a Skib, Skip, Fegattskib, or more commonly called a Full Rigger. All these names meant the same thing, the way in which the ship was outfitted. The *Norske Love* was square rigged with three large masts. Each mast proudly waved square crisp white sails that snapped in the wind. The crew consisted of sixteen hearty souls and the captain. Captain Bentsen had sailed across the Atlantic many times and was considered to be a God-fearing, honest, vivacious man. He loved the sea, and he loved his *Norske Love*. This was his home.

"It is a good sign, the name of our ship. The *Norske Love*," Hans said as he squeezed his eldest child to his side. "Our ancestors where Norske Vikings. Brave and strong. We must carry on the tradition as well. Can you be brave and strong for the little ones, Mary Jane?"

Mary Jane lovingly looked up into her father's smiling face. It was obvious he was thrilled with the adventure that was laid out in front of them. His gray eyes twinkled, and the dimple on his left cheek winked at her as he grinned.

"Yes, Papa. I will help Mama with the little ones. And I will be proud to continue the family tradition. I will be a brave and strong Viking, without the pillaging and plundering, of course." Mary Jane laughed.

Hans again gave his daughter a squeeze as he laughed at her humor. Often, he found himself amazed at Mary Jane's sharp mind and her quick wit. Is it possible that she was already fifteen years old? If they were to stay in Oslo, Sweden, he had no doubt that that tall blonde boy would have asked for her hand in marriage. Hans would have said yes. The match would have been a good one for Mary Jane. Bertha was fifteen when they had wed. It was time.

How would things change for Mary Jane in America? he thought to himself.

Again, Hans looked down at his daughter. Her thick long auburn hair was blowing in the breeze. She had her mother's eyes, but the green orbs of her eyes where surrounded by the thickest eyelashes Hans had ever seen. Mary Jane had a splattering of freckled across her nose that still gave her an impish appearance. But when she smiled, there was no longer any trace of a child. She was now a beautiful young woman. Smart, strong with just the right amount of sass. He again hugged her lovingly to his side, proud to be her papa.

Hans and Bertha Nilsson and their ten children were joined with forty-one members from the church, including Pastor Dom. With the fifty-three Swedish immigrants, the crew, and the captain, the *Norske Love* was packed full for her trip across the north Atlantic, some of the most treacherous water on earth. The human cargo was, however, not the only cargo that was loaded aboard in Sweden. Iron from Swedish mines to be delivered to New York City was Captain Bentsen's main payload. This iron would be used in building more rail lines to accommodate the northern industries and to provide transportation for Union soldiers and materials. All for the northern cause.

"We have nothing to fear," Pastor Dom had informed the congregation. "The war between the states is being fought in the Southern states. We will disembark in New York City. From there, we will travel by rail to the Mississippi River and up into Minnesota. Miles and miles from the conflict. Nothing to fear."

There was, of course, a lot to fear with such a voyage. The trip over was not nearly as hazardous as it had been for early Swedish immigrants in the late seventeenth century. Still, it was a dangerous and uncomfortable two months at sea. The wooden bunks below deck were eight-feet wide and could uncomfortably hold five passengers. Bertha Nilsson had insisted that the Nilsson family would share two adjoining bunks. This provided a small corner of the ship for the family's privacy. This added cost, along with the adult fair of 90 crooner ($20 US dollars) made the voyage very costly for such a large family. Hans Nilsson had been a very successful stonemason in Sweden and was frugal with his money. He had been planning and saving for the trip to America for years. They had sold everything they owned, and it would take almost every cent to get to Minnesota.

The first railroads lines were laid in the United States in the early 1830s. So the rail lines in the Northern states were quite extensive by 1862, and more were being laid down daily to accommodate the war efforts. One line would carry the immigrants from New York City to Chicago. From Chicago, another would take them to the banks of the Mississippi River. Here, they would board a Stern Wheeler that would take them to Minneapolis and their new home, the state of Minnesota. In Minneapolis, Hans would have to purchase a team of strong horses and a sturdy wagon and, of course, the supplies he would need to begin their new life, build their home, and plant their first crops. They would be farmers now. Farmers and of course he still had the skill and reputation of being an excellent rock mason. Hans hoped to make money at the trade he loved. After all, everyone needed a fireplace. Didn't they?

"And don't you forget, Hans Nilsson," Bertha had said at least a hundred times, "I'll be wanting a glass window in my new home in America."

Hans would not forget.

The Minnesota War

LITTLE CROWS RAIDING party was successful. They returned before daybreak without any bloodshed, which made Wabasha give thanks to the great creator. Bread, blankets, and clothing were what they were able to pass out to the People. Bacon was also distributed, but there was not enough to go around. It was obvious that another raid would be needed.

Scouts watched the city for months and did not report any concerning build up of military might. One scout did report a wagon shipment of supplies being stored in a warehouse at the far end of town. The crates were all marked with their destination, Fort Snelling. Fort Snelling was the nearest military strong hold and was within a half a day's walk from the twin cities. Little did the Natives know that Fort Snelling and its recruitments were responsible for protecting the settlers in Minnesota. As the Civil War continued, Fort Snelling was now the location for the necessary training for thousands of Minnesota volunteers who would be serving in the Union army.

Chief Little Crow began to plan his next raid. As the sun arose, the Sioux would attack. Their goal was the storage warehouse outside of town. Again, Chief Little Crow would lead his men to glory. The excitement rose within his chest. Sleep slowly overswept him as he dreamed of victory.

In the predawn darkness, five hundred Santee Sioux broke into the food warehouse. Floor to ceiling, the wooden crates were stacked. Flour, sugar, coffee, tobacco, and dried meat. It was more than Little Crow had expected and would be enough to see his people through another harsh Minnesota winter that was rapidly approaching. The warriors worked rapidly, loading what they could on horseback. Crates were smashed opened and left in a heap on the wooden floor. Dozens and dozens of loaded horses had already left heading back across the plains in the dark for the Indian encampment along Sand Creek. Little Crow and his men were almost finished.

Another successful raid, Little Crow thought to himself.

His need to provide his people with winter supplies was met, but he still felt an insatiable hunger for revenge. Revenge for those people lost, for broken treaties, and for promises never fulfilled.

❖ Mary Jane ❖

General John Pope sat atop his painted mare, assessing the Natives as they quietly slithered out of town, so quickly they seemed unburdened by the hundreds of pounds of United States military supplies they were stealing. They were nothing more than vermin.

"It is my purpose to utterly exterminate the Sioux. They are to be treated as maniacs or wild beasts and by no means as people with whom treaties or compromises can be made." Pope had once stated these words to a comrade. And with the backing of the White House and his high-powered father, who was to stand in his way?

Little Crow watched with pride as his people moved efficiently and quietly, knowing the importance of their task at hand. The first shot rang through the warehouse and sent a shiver down his spine. This was the moment he had been waiting for.

With a wave of his right arm, General Pope gave the signal, and the flood gates were opened. Hundreds of United States Calvary rushed in on horseback. Blue uniforms surrounded the warehouse while shots rang out from all directions. The raiding party was overwhelmed by the military might and sheer number of soldiers. Some soldiers were obviously well trained; some were, however, very new to the battlefield. Few did not even speak English, being new immigrants here for the promise of a bright future in America. But before their future could begin, the Indian's existence needed to end. All in the name of progress and civilization.

Prisoners of war were taken to Fort Snelling, where they were held for questioning. By October, snow covered the fields outside and the floors of the cells. Little Crow's breath hung heavy in front of his face as he spoke through the iron bars to his people.

"Do not lose heart. We did what any white man would do, we fed our people."

Military trials began, each lasting ten to fifteen minutes, in which the warriors were charged with theft, rape, and murder. Three hundred and three Sioux men were found guilty and sentenced to death. The Minnesota authorities, including General Pope, were hungry for blood and wanted every one of them executed by hanging. Far too many settlers had been robbed and even killed in Minnesota. It would be close to impossible to encourage others to move to this isolated state if the Indian problem could not be controlled. This was the time. It was crucial. A solution must be found and swiftly executed.

The Civil War had dragged on long enough. Months longer than any one in Washington could have foreseen. The death tolls were staggering, and the President demanded that all steps must be made to ensure that the end was not only victorious for the Union but also in the very near future. There was just not enough funds or manpower to continue to battle Natives and rebels simultaneously.

President Abraham Lincoln was concerned about rumors drifting across the Atlantic Ocean. European powers had threatened to support the Confederate cause if such brutal actions culminated. The White House intervened with a solution—a bargain. The White House administration was able to trim the execution list down to forty men. All of whom were found guilty of excessive brutality against white settlers and damage or loss of property belonging to the United States Government. This list included Chief Little Crow for the attack at the warehouse. This list also included Chief Wabasha, a man who had devoted his entire life to establish a peaceful coexistence with the whites.

General Pope was disgusted with these numbers and demanded free reign at removing every last Native from the state. His state. His connections again will have a strong impact on history. He and his army were given two million dollars in addition to the right to use any force deemed necessary to eradicate all Indians from the glorious Empire State of Minnesota. Eradicate, to rid Minnesota of all Natives, by any means deemed fit. To chase off, relocate, or even kill—that was left up to the general.

The first order of business was the young arrogant and aggressive Chief Little Crow. The evening of December 18, the water froze in the troughs. Union men huddled around small fires in their barracks; it was too cold to sleep. This provided time for them to debate, argue, and plan.

"Hanging is too good for the like of those heathen devils!" spat one young lieutenant. Several nods around the room proved he was not the only soldier who felt this way. But the law was the law, even in this wilderness.

In the prison cells, with open bars on the windows, with no heat and only one small woolen blanket, the Sioux prisoners prayed for the sunrise and some relief from the bitter cold. In the early morning hours, it was discovered that Chief Little Crow was not in his cell. The door was locked, but the prisoner was nowhere to be found. A quiet search ensued. Was it possible he escaped? No. The fort was too well guarded.

Several soldiers were questioned, but they remained quiet. If they knew something, they were not sharing it with their commanding officers.

The cold continued to punish the inhabitants of Fort Snelling, while preparations were being made for the public execution. Early the next morning, Little Crow was discovered. His mutilated body was found outside of the fort walls in frozen pieces. The brutality in which he was murdered shook even the hardiest soldiers to their core. His escape and brutal death would never be completely explained.

On December 26, 1862, President Lincoln ordered the largest mass execution in American history. The streets of Mankato, Minnesota, were flooded with eager witnesses. Thirty-nine Sioux men, including Wabasha, were hung in the town square with General Pope proudly overseeing the entire affair.

"We are now one step closer to bringing civilization to the beautiful state of Minnesota," Pope boasted while the bodies still hung from the gallows.

Many white settlers felt relief. Relief that the Indian conflict was finally over.

But was it?

Many were friends of the Natives, mainly the northern tribe of Chippewa that they had been trading with for years. The question floated throughout these few groups, Was guilt determined beyond a reasonable doubt? It did not matter. The Minnesota War was over. The time of peace between the Native people was now a distant and painful memory.

Life at Sea

SURVIVING TWO MONTHS on board the *Norske Love* seemed like a daunting task. Illness and even deaths were common place. The crowded living conditions made cleanliness and sanitation a daily struggle. But young Mary Jane surprised herself and found the voyage exhilarating. Each morning, she crawled over the sleeping bodies of her younger siblings to stroll on deck. The mornings were her favorite. It was still and quiet, with only a few deck hands mulling about. Captain Bentsen was at the wheel without fail. He had long since become accustomed to Mary Jane's early morning ritual and looked forward to their silent mornings together.

The misty gray sky melted into the sea. The two becoming one. As Mary Jane grasped the weathered railing, she squinted her eyes to catch the first glimpse of separation between sky and sea. The sea-weathered wood was smooth and sturdy under her slender fingers. She traced the now familiar grooves in the banister, patiently waiting. When the sun peeked its head above the horizon, the first tentacles of light reached across the breath of the Atlantic Ocean. The morning light turning the misty gray sky into a moist peach curtain of uncertainty. Well worth the wait.

Somewhere out there was land. A huge vast piece of land that held Mary Jane's future. All their futures. Every day, she got closer. Every day, her anticipation grew. What would this new land look like? The elders in her church group had said it would be covered with vast forests as far as the eye could see. That the rivers were so full of fish, you would not have to bait a hook. You just scooped them up with your bare hands. So many fish that you could walk across the river on their backs with our getting your feet wet. That the soil was so fertile, that plants grew without seeds being sown. And cows grew as fat as elephants. Could any land be that spectacular? Mary Jane doubted much of what they said, but she still could not wait to view it with her own eyes.

She and her siblings had been passing the time aboard the ship with their studies. Papa wanted his children to speak English. The only books they had that were written in English was a copy of Homer's *Odyssey* and a tattered Bible. Mary Jane had studied English in her one room school house in Orsa, Sweden. She was actually quite good with the complicated language and felt stronger with it daily, using small conversations with the sailors to assist her. Teaching her little brothers and sisters was a different story.

Nettie was picking up well with her English lessons. But she was almost fourteen years old and had also studied English in school before they left Sweden. Eric was next, and at twelve years old, he believed he already knew enough English. Alfred was almost eleven years old and loved anything to do with school. Al would probably be able to speak English better than Mary Jane before they reached New York. Henry was nine and was only interested in the more colorful language spoken by the sailors, much to Mama's dismay. Little Christina was seven. She had difficulty reading Swedish, so Mama was working with her on that issue. Then there were the five-year-old twins, George and Isaar. They were a handful—well, two hands full. They spent most of their time playing marbles on the bunk. At least then, it was known they were not diving over the side of the ship into the sea. The babies spent most of their day also in the bunk with Mama. Charlie who was a big boy at three, and then the baby. The baby was called Baby Boy by everyone except Mama. Bertha Nilsson called her youngest child by his given name Jonathon. Mary Jane wondered how much of this voyage the younger children would remember.

The days melded into one long nonending blur. The only respite for Mary Jane was her morning ritual to the deck above to watch the sunrise with Captain Bentsen. This morning, when she arrived above deck, she could tell something was different immediately. The deck was organized chaos. Men scrambled to and fro. Orders, directions, and mist washed over her.

"You better get below, miss," said one sailor.

"A storm approaches fast!" His outstretched arm and finger pointed toward the western horizon when an ominous dark cloud rapidly approached. "Tell the others to prepare." With that, the sailor scrambled off, obeying an order that was barked to him by the captain himself.

Mary Jane quickly scurried down the narrow stairs to the steerage level where the immigrants were just stirring.

"Papa, a storm is coming. They sent me down to tell you to prepare for it," she whispered, fear obvious in her strained voice.

Hans Nilsson tussled his daughter's hair and gave her a forced smile. "We better do as the captain orders then. Wake the others."

If above deck was organized chaos, below deck was the exact opposite. Fear was on every face as members from the congregation began to stow belongings safely away.

"Nothing should be lost," Papa directed.

Nets were strapped around luggage, and Papa's toolbox was carefully stowed below the bunk and strapped in. Everything the family owned was neatly tucked into one small corner. Mama made the bunks, then ordered all the children to sit and begin their studies. She quickly made a small bowl of porridge, then poured water into the cook stove, putting the small flame out. The bowl was passed around. Each child ate from the same pot using the same wooden spoon. The meal was over only minutes before the first wave came.

The ship was tossed up in the air like a toy. As the *Norske Love* slid down the other side of the monster wave, everyone slid to the port side. The storm continued throughout the day and into the night. It was impossible to sleep. The babies cried, and the younger children trembled with fear. Several small injuries occurred, mostly bumps and bruises. Old Mrs. Oslow fell off her bunk, broke her wrist, and bruised her side. Hans Nilsson worried she may have broken a rib. It was difficult for Mrs. Oslow to take a deep breath. Mrs. Oslow was the midwife, and her knowledge of medical care was impressive. She knew how badly she was injured but kept that information to herself. Mary Jane tended her as best she could.

Bertha Nilsson was not faring any better. She could not stop vomiting. She had not informed her family yet. Perhaps she was hoping she was wrong. But she was not. Mama was pregnant. This would be her eleventh child. Within hours, Mama's skin was the same dull gray color as the dim light below decks. The storm raged on. Waves angrily slapped at the sides of the ship, threatening to rip the *Norse Love* in two. Rainwater mixed with sea and washed down the narrow stairs into the immigrants' compartment. Frigid water rose to ankle deep. Everything and everyone was wet, cold, and miserable. Mary Jane prayed they would survive the voyage.

Finally, on the second day, the storm broke. The rain stopped, and the waves were tolerable. The wind was now against them, more than usual.

"This will extend the trip another several days, maybe a week," Papa said. During the last week of the voyage, the wind stopped almost completely.

A doldrum, the captain called it.

By this time, the supplies were dangerously low. Fresh water was rationed to each passenger, a tablespoon at a time. Pickled eggs were the only food left. Mary Jane swore she would never eat another pickled egg. She could hardly stand the smell of them.

Mrs. Oslow's arm was not healing well. Her side was now a purple greenish color and was so tender to the touch. Mary Jane watched tears stream quietly down her wrinkled cheeks as she changed her bandage wrappings. But it was the lack of water that proved to be too much for her body to take. Somewhere between the setting of the sun and the early morning hours, she took her last raspy breath, while the rest of them slept.

A burial at sea was like nothing Mary Jane had witnessed before. The women carefully washed Mrs. Oslow, while the men and boys waited above deck. They dressed her in her cleanest garments. A wooden cross on twine was lovingly tied to her neck by Bertha Nilsson herself. Her hair was combed again, and then she was wrapped from head to toe in the same canvas that was used to mend the sails.

"Tie that Mary Jane, would you?" asked Mama.

Mary Jane was given twine and expected to tie it around Mrs. Oslow's feet. The thought of the task made Mary Jane's stomach flip twice. She closed her eyes and took a deep, cleansing breath. Remembering the kind smile and gentle touch of this lovely woman, Mary Jane opened her eyes. This time, they filled with tears. Tenderly, she lifted Mrs. Oslow's bound feet and secured the canvas with the twine offered by her mother.

"That's my girl," Mama cooed, running her hand down the length of Mary Jane's dark hair. "Thank you, bobbin." The nickname was usually spoken only by her father, but Mary Jane looked into her mothers eyes and silently thanked her for the endearing support.

Captain Bentsen oversaw the burial. After the pastor read from the Bible and said more than a few words about the kind and gentle heart that was now residing with the Lord, he followed an ancient Swedish custom. Mrs. Oslow's bread ration for the day was laid upon the cocoon that capsulated the woman who would never see the shores of America. As the pastor reached for the dry crusty, token he spoke. "With this, I take on any sin. So this soul may rest in peace in the arms of glory."

Quietly, he chewed, then swallowed. A pewter mug of tepid water was handed to him, and he drank deeply. With that, Mrs. Oslow was ready for her journey.

The captain gave the quiet command. Two sailors lifted Mrs. Oslow's body to the ship's railing, the same railing that had given Mary Jane so much comfort in the early morning hours. With a nod of the captain's head, Mrs. Oslow slipped over the side of the ship, into the dark water below. Mary Jane peered over the side as the canvas bundle slipped beneath the waves and disappeared forever.

Food and water was still heavily rationed. Mary Jane could not quench her thirst, and salty tears did not help the matter. The passengers were stoic for the rest of the voyage. American shores could not be close enough.

Anishinabe The People

CHIEF CRANE OF the Chippewa watched the sun set over the Red Lake. His heart was heavy. A single tear ran down his strong cheek and disappeared into the collar of his cotton shirt. What will happen to his people now? Since the execution of the Sioux warriors down south, he dreaded what was coming. The white population in Minnesota had exploded. Cities were sprouting from the earth like spring grass. Everywhere. Wagon tracks could be seen no matter where he walked. Migratory paths and hunting grounds where disappearing thanks to barbed-wire fencing that marked land now considered to belong to the white settlers.

The great Chippewa Chief did not mourn the loss of the Sioux warriors. They had been his enemies for many moons. He mourned the loss of security and freedom that his people will now surely be stripped of. The white leaders did not see the difference between tribes. They did not care that Chippewa were not Sioux. They would not remember the friendships and kindnesses shared throughout the years between the Chippewa and the whites. All they would see is Indians. Indians that were in their way.

A meeting had already been called for. General Pope wished the chiefs from the seven clans of the Red Lake Chippewa to meet at Fort Snelling. They would be leaving in the morning.

The sky was now pink and orange. Colors streaked across the heavens as if they had been painted by the creators hand itself. Chief Crane closed his eyes and inhaled deeply. The scent of pine filled his nostrils. The pine forests that surrounded this territory were of great value to the United States Government. It would be only a matter of time that this land would no longer be the home of the Anishinabe, the People. Perhaps a matter of months or even days. Chief Crane knew in his heart that this is why the meeting had been called. Another treaty. Another opportunity for the white mans words to trick and confuse the People.

The Chippewa or Ojibwa, as they preferred, had not always lived around the Great Lakes. They were members of an ancient Algonquin people from the great saltwater to the east, the Atlantic Coast. The people had moved west to escape hostile tribes centuries ago when great glaciers marked a northern boundary. Chief Crane had heard the elders tell the tales around the fires his entire life.

When the People walked into these northern woods, they knew they had found their new home. The migration had been prophesized to end where they found food that grew on water. Wild rice. As gatherers, they collected berries, nuts, and harvested the rice early each fall. As hunters, they followed their prey but never strayed too far from the heart of their territory. The shores of the lakes and the home of the wild rice.

On a map in Washington, DC, imaginary lines were drawn, displaying the Chippewa Territory as covering northern Minnesota and North Dakota up into Canada. This included the western boundary of Lake Superior. Red Lake sat almost dead center. The heart of the People's territory. Chief Crane could not see these lines as he watched the pink sky turn to a warm amber. But he knew this territory well. He knew where the elk migrated to calve. He knew where the maple trees were, and when to harvest their sweet sap. He knew where the wild rice grew and where the big fish were hiding along the shady bank of the rivers. He knew where the People gathered for their annual celebration of life ceremony. Where they danced through the night to the beat of the drum, the heartbeat of the earth, praising the creator for the many gifts this land has bestowed upon the People. And he knew where the bones of his ancestors were buried. The ancient trails were difficult for others to see, but not Chief Crane. He could visualize them now on the back of his eyelids. These lines were carved into his very soul.

He slowly opened his eyes and was greeted with the final kiss of the day. The sun dipped west behind the hills, but the orange and pink swirls still decorated the sky. The torches were being lit along the banks of the lake for night fishing. His people would harvest many fat trout tonight. They would feast, laugh, and dance. The drum would beat to honor our ancestors and pray for their guidance at the treaty meeting.

Chief Crane squared his shoulders and pulled himself up to his full impressive height. His people will be looking to him tonight for guidance and hope for their future. He must deliver. His long strides swiftly covered the ground back into camp, where he could hear preparations for tonight's event. He heard children laugh, a woman was singing as a baby cooed in response. He looked around his camp, with one long, sweeping glance. A tightness in his chest restricted his breathing. That was a feeling he had been accustomed to since the meeting at the sacred Red Rock Quarry. Tonight, his mind and spirit were in agreement, and this weighed heavy on a man responsible for the safety of so many. Chief Crane knew that this would be the very last evening his people would ever see and feel complete and total freedom.

Arrival 1863

THE HISTORY OF New York City was well established by 1863. Mary Jane heard even more from the sailors as land fall finally approached. The territory that was known as New York had been occupied by a variety of Native American tribes for thousands of years. Several European explores claimed the glory of discovering this fertile landscape, but in actuality, it was an Italian explorer hired by the French government named Giovanni de Verrazano who arrived in the New York Bay back in 1524. He will be the first to report its splendors to Europe.

The area was heavily populated by natives that had established a tranquil life amongst the sea and fertile land. Hunting and fishing was plentiful, and the landscape had to have been breathtaking. Then in 1609, an English explorer named Henry Hudson stumbled upon the area while he was searching for a direct waterway to Asia and the Orient, infamously known as the North West Passage.

The first colony was established by the Dutch, however, in 1625. They immediately prospered thanks entirely to a friendly trade relationship with the thousands of natives that called this territory home and had for thousands of years. The temperate climate, long-growing season, and bountiful land promised a prosperous existence. The colony was named New Amsterdam. The Dutch West India Company who actually sent these colonist barely survived their first winter.

Local Native Americans aided the starving settlers by taking them to their hunting grounds, Manhattan. On the island of Manhattan, game was plentiful, fishing was easy, and shell fish was bountiful. Within just a few weeks, they had gathered enough supplies and food to see them through another New Amsterdam winter. Metal coins, trinkets, and jewelry were given to the natives for their assistance.

The following hunting season, when the natives returned to Manhattan, they were not greeted by friendly faces like they had anticipated. Instead, they found a wooded wall and sharp hostility keeping them from their hunting grounds. The trinkets exchanged were apparently not given in gratitude. According to the Dutch, Manhattan had been purchased. Natives were no longer welcome. This was known as the Manhattan land sale, the most plentiful hunting grounds on the east coast of America, purchased for the equivalent of twenty-four gold coins.

New Amsterdam will flourish until it will be traded for by the British and renamed New York. New York will be America's largest and most important sea port for many years through the Revolutionary War and the War of 1812. It was no different today.

The seaport looked more like a forest. A forest of ship masts. Hundreds of masts reached to the heavens. The harbor was choked with Riggers, Schooners, and Clipper Ships of all shapes and sizes. Sails snapped in the wind as did flags of every color, representing the countries that controlled the vessels and crew.

Mary Jane stood in her favorite spot, grasping the now very familiar wooden banister. Her fingers tracing the smooth grain of the weathered wood fondly.

"Did you know that New York City was once America's capital?" Captain Bentsen's voice was as smooth as the ship rail Mary Jane clasped.

"No. Really?" she replied, interested.

"Yes. It truly was," he continued. His deep voice gripped Mary Jane's attention.

"George Washington even took his oath as our first president in this city. Over there," he said, pointing toward the southern tip of the island. "On the balcony of Federal Hall. It was 1789, I think. After the Revolutionary War was over. It was short-lived. Now the capital is Washington, DC, down south of us here." With that, the history lesson was over. The captain's attention was needed elsewhere. Mary Jane fell into her comfortable silence, observing every thing around her.

"Over there," she muttered to herself as she peered over the railing to take a closer look at the city of New York as the *Norske Love* slowly came into the harbor and prepared to dock.

New York was teeming with buildings. Some looked to be almost four stories tall. Several were elegant Brownstown buildings with colossal arches and decorative leaded glass windows. The majority of the buildings was made of wood, clapboard, and shared a wall with their neighbor. Awnings and signs called to the passerby to come in take a look at the merchants' wares. The noises and the smells enthralled Mary Jane. Men shouted from crows nests and rigging. Docks were a blur of activity, and the street that ran parallel to the shore line was packed with people, horses, and carriages. Fresh baked bread mingled with the salt from the sea and gave the fishy smell of the harbor a delicious aroma.

Mary Jane felt heady as she carefully soaked it all in. This was America. The land so many dreamed of. The land so many sacrificed to see, and she was finally here.

Some of the streets in New York City were paved with cobblestone, while others were packed dirt. Wooden elevated sidewalks provided pedestrians walking space along the wharf. There was mud and manure everywhere. But the New Yorkers seemed not to mind either. People bustled to and fro, carrying out their daily tasks. Horse-drawn carriages, trolleys, and ferry boats provided transportation, but most traveled by foot. The energy delighted Mary Jane.

Along the wharf, men, women, and children sold pies, fresh fruit, fish, flowers, and fresh vegetables. One man with a large red cart was selling hot corn on the cob. The smell made Mary Jane's stomach growl after so many days of small rations. This was downtown New York City. Mary Jane's first taste of America.

Uptown was quite different. Sprawling farms and large uncultivated tracts of land covered the island and mainland alike. Swaying trees surrounded by a spattering of rocky outcrops framed several bubbling streams and natural springs. Small villages dotted the landscape, making good use of the areas natural splendors. The population was growing rapidly with so many immigrants coming into the harbor. New York City was beginning to break into boroughs, small areas or neighborhoods. Here, immigrants tended to stick together, with people from their homeland. People that shared their same customs, traditions, and languages.

"Mary Jane." Papa laid his arm around his daughter's slender shoulders. "Come down and help your mama get the little ones ready, please. Hurry. We need to be moving fast today." Bertha Nilsson was having a difficult pregnancy, no doubt in part to the over sea voyage and lack of fresh food and water these past two months. Mary Jane was taking on more and more duties with her younger siblings, anything to help. But it was obvious that everyone feared for Mama's health as well as the unborn child's. As Mary Jane went below decks, Hans disappeared into the crowd of men talking with Pastor Dom and the captain.

"You must move through the city as rapidly as possible." Captain Bentsen was talking with his hands, more animated than anyone had seen prior on the voyage.

"Stop for nothing. You must make haste." His voice was heavy with urgency.

Congress had recently actively enforced the draft. Every able body male above the age of eighteen was eligible. With so many immigrants entering the United States through the New York City harbor, it was a prime location for Union soldiers to gather up new recruits. Many would be drafted the same day they stepped off the ship.

In the early summer of 1863, the commutation fee was also introduced. A wealthy member of society could pay the US Government $300 to be excluded from the draft. This led to tensions among New Yorkers, mainly fresh immigrants who did not have two pennies to rub together, let alone three hundred dollars. The idea that war was for the poor was not a favorable one on the streets of New York.

"You must gather your families and board the train immediately," the captain continued. A trusted deckhand was on his way to the train station to ascertain when the next train to Chicago would leave the station.

"Stay aboard the ship until the last possible moment. Then split up into small groups. This will draw less attention to you. Make your way to the station and speak to no one." The lack of English spoken by the immigrants only divulged their newness to America and the fact these men were not yet enlisted into the military.

President Abraham Lincoln had sent several regiments of militia and volunteer troops into the heart of New York City to control the largest civil insurrection in American history, second only to the Civil War itself. A violent Irish mob had recently ransacked buildings and set fire to numerous homes and shops. The dry wooden structures went up in flames that rapidly consumed them and spread uncontrollably throughout the city. What began as a cry against unjust economic division soon took an ugly racial turn. Within days, the rioters focused their angry attentions onto black New Yorkers. Black citizens were targeted and blamed for the war in its entirety. Eleven men where lynched in the streets, and countless others were harassed and tormented. The black population was forced into hiding with in their own city limits. The final blow was when the rioters set fire to a black orphanage on Front Street. Hundreds of now homeless children fled into the streets and alleyways.

The mob was finally suppressed by the military and their uses of artillery and fixed bayonets. The death toll was staggering, and the tension was still palatable along the wharf and streets of the great city.

The next train leaving the station was not heading directly to Chicago. It was going to the city of Albany, New York. It was decided that this was the safest and quickest route out of New York City and away from the Union draft board. The immigrants said their farewells, and as soon as the sun sank below the horizon, they boarded the train. The rail car was full. Seating on the floor in the steerage car was all that was available and affordable for most immigrants. It was by no means a comfortable way to travel, but comfort had been elusive the past few months. What was a few more days of it? Mary Jane's back ached as she leaned against the wooden wall of the rail car. A curly head of a sleeping twin laid on each of her knees. She closed her eyes and prayed for sleep to over take her. She would not have to wait long.

Once they arrived in Albany, they boarded a passenger boat, really a ferry. The ferry took the family up the Erie Canal to Buffalo, New York. Here, they saw the glorious Niagara Falls. Mary Jane had never seen such a beautiful sight. Her enthusiasm returned full heartedly. America was spectacular.

The Erie Canal was built in 1825, a joint effort of several New York businessmen and the taxpayers, of course. The Erie Canal connected the cities of Albany and Buffalo, New York. But more importantly, it connected Lake Erie to the Hudson River and then the New York Harbor. Some believed digging a ditch 363 miles was pure folly, including former President Thomas Jefferson. But New Yorkers proceeded with the task and the trade route, a shortcut that proved to be a huge and very profitable success. America's first and most famous canal.

In Buffalo, the Nilssons boarded another train taking them through Chicago and onto Rock Island where the tracks stopped at the banks of the Mississippi River. Here they took one of the few steam boats that had not been commissioned by the Union army. This steamboat carried freight and passengers as well, north to St. Anthony Falls and the city of St. Paul. The entire excursion from New York City to St. Paul was an exhausting eleven days. But they were finally here, Minnesota. Their new home.

The Old Crossing Treaty

THE LEAVES WERE turning orange and yellow. The brilliant colors blanketed the rolling hills outside of Fort Snelling. The afternoon was still and warm. Unseasonably warm for early fall. Teepees were neatly arranged outside of the safety of the fort walls, while the soldier barracks were neatly arranged inside the walls. Both military sides demonstrated a well-organized battalion of warriors. The tension was high, making it difficult for even the animals to breath comfortably.

The Union horses were tethered to posts, while the Chippewa horses stood erect, ready to obey any command from their master. Blankets were set in a semicircle on the dry grass for the Indian chiefs. A long wooden table was set up at the northern end of the circle, elevated on a two-foot-high stage. It was here that General Pope and his comrades sat looking down on the great chiefs of the Chippewa nation.

"All Dakota land is forfeit," General Pope growled.

His blue uniform was freshly laundered, and his brass buttons, polished. They glinted in the afternoon sun like drops of gold. His army hat shaded his eyes, but Chief Crane knew what they looked like without seeing them this day. They would be sharp and shrewd like an owl, ready to swoop down on his small and insignificant prey. That is what the People were to Pope, small and insignificant.

"This land now belongs to the United States Government and any US citizen claiming residence." This equaled over eleven million acres. Tribal acres. This treaty would supersede any and all previous treaties that had promised the Red Lake Territory to the Chippewa People. Pope paused, and his eyes locked with Chief Cranes, then he continued without wavering his steely stare.

"Under the order of President Lincoln and the United States Government, the Chippewa people will be paid $500,000 for lands in the northwest region of Minnesota. You will vacate this territory. Immediately."

The crowd erupted. Indians jumped to their feet pounding their fists in the air.

"This land is *not* for sale," one angry warrior yelled.

"Red Lake is ours. You cannot just take it!" cried another.

As the voices grew in strength, soldiers stepped forward with their hands on their weapons, ready for anything. Some even looking forward to it. Chief Crane slowly stood. He was silent and still. Then he took two large, purposeful strides toward the podium where he stopped, looking up directly at General Pope. The voices all quieted instantly. Chief Crane's ears rang with the sound of his own heartbeat. He inhaled slowly, calming the urge to jump on the podium and wring the neck of the pompous General Pope.

"And what if we do not agree to this proposal." It was a statement, not a question. His voice was steady and strong. His people standing behind him spoke not a word. They waited, holding their breath.

"You do not have a choice, Crane," spat General Pope.

"This is the way it is. This is the way it will be—"

"Or?" interrupted Chief Crane.

"Or it will end like it did with the Sioux," Pope finished. His eyes were easy to read now. Chief Crane was correct. They did have the appearance of a hungry owl.

The Old Crossing Treaty of 1863 will be remembered as one of the most corrupt land deals in history. Land that had been given to the natives in several earlier treaties was now being taken away. No money would ever trade hands, and Pope knew it would be this way. The Chippewa Indians were being punished. Punished for the wrongdoings of the Sioux Tribe. Punished for the Minnesota War. Punished for being Indian.

Minnesota

S T. PAUL, the capital city of Minnesota, was located along the shore of the great Mississippi River. At this time, the population was mostly Catholic immigrants from European countries. The Scandinavian immigrants were part of a new group of Christians in America—Baptists. They were unwelcome in much of St. Paul with the exception of their pocketbook. They stayed in town only long enough to ascertain strong horses, a sturdy wagon and whatever supplies they would need to begin building their homestead and new life in Minnesota. Hans Nilsson was well organized and efficient about gathering the necessary supplies to set up his family's new homestead. He purchased lumber, shingles, equipment, and seeds. He did not forget his wife's glass window.

The Nilsson family was exhausted from their journey. Two months at sea, then an eleven-day dash across the nation from New York to Minnesota. Mary Jane had now been aboard a sea vessel, a paddle wheeler, steam-powered locomotive, and now a wagon train that would carry her north toward the Red Lake area and their new home. The extreme fatigue weighed heaviest on Bertha Nilsson. Now with Bertha in her sixth month of pregnancy, Hans worried for her health and the health of his unborn child.

Bertha was thin and frail. The light from her eyes shone no more. Her skin had taken on a gray pallor, and dark circles under her eyes gave her the appearance of a feeble raccoon. Even her voice sounded fatigued. Hans looked for a doctor in St. Paul to give her and the baby a thorough examination.

For two dollars, Dr. Amstand told them to boil some rusty nails and to have Bertha drink the water from the concoction after it had cooled.

"This will help her anemia," he proclaimed. Hans was not assured, but they did what the doctor ordered. The family, along with the immigrants, had gathered outside of town and put up a temporary shelter. Here, Bertha rested, while Mary Jane tended the children, and Hans and the other men gathered supplies and readied the wagons for the last leg of their arduous voyage.

The economic boom and America's prosperous era of the 1800s had come to a close as the Civil War dragged on. Now banks and insurance companies failed in the east and were calling in their loans. The Midwest was hit hard. Many could not pay off their loans. Several difficult years followed, ensuring that virtually, no money was flowing in territories like the new state of Minnesota. The immigrants were plagued with offers and "good deals" left and right. It was a bit overwhelming.

Hans was very frugal with his money and had purchased what he needed and was anxious to move on long before the others. That night, it was decided that his family would set off at sunrise. The other would follow days behind them.

The St. Paul assayer's office sold the Nilssons a map of the territory and helped Hans locate his parcel of 140 acres. It was just south of Red Lake. By his calculations, it would take them at least three days to reach it by wagon.

"Three days through hostile Indian Territory," the assayer had said.

"These savages were ordered to relocate north, but not all of 'em follow the law. What can you expect? We hung a bunch of murderin' savages here a few months ago. Now they are all on the war path," the assayer added. "Devils! All of 'em!"

They followed the Mississippi River north. The river was wide and moved slowly. Brambles of twigs and debris drifted by. Mary Jane found the smell of the river and the constant gurgle of it soothing. Minnesota was beautiful. The rolling hills were covered with brush and deciduous trees that were losing their colorful leaves. Pine tree forests dotted the landscape north. They traveled past dozens of pristine blue lakes that were a direct result of Minnesota's glacial past.

The water was crystal clear; the fish was plentiful. The stories of America's splendor were true. It was really a land of plenty.

Bertha and the smaller children rode in the back of the wagon. Mary Jane sat on the buck board next to her father, not wanting to miss a thing. They were regularly joined by one of the older children who also enjoyed the view from the front.

At night, they slept under the stars along the bank of the river, talking of what their land would look like. Certainly, it would be as spectacular as what they have already seen. On the third day, they reached a small community, the town of Brainerd. This would be their town. Their homestead was on the northern outskirts.

Brainerd was a small river town that served the needs of hundreds of farmers that lived in its surrounding territory. The town was built on one street that overlooked the Mississippi River. The elevated wooden sidewalk offered pedestrians a small amount of reprisal from the dirt, mud, and manure that made up the street itself. The town consisted of a row of wooden buildings, all thirsty for a new coat of paint. At the far end was a livery stable with a busy black smith at the forge, then a saloon with large swinging doors. Across a small alley way was a restaurant with two large glass windows in front and what appeared to be hotel rooms on the second floor. This building shared a wall with the telegraph office that also served as the post office. The last building on the street was the mercantile. Bertha insisted on visiting the mercantile where they introduced themselves to the store's owner and his wife. In this one room, they sold everything a body could want. There were rakes and shovels, guns and knives, jams and preserves, gloves and hats, and even a pretty blue dress and bonnet in the window.

On the back wall was the town's message board. Notices were posted of land and horses for sale, a job opening, and an announcement of the last church picnic of the year. There were also three tin-type photos of young men in their military uniforms. They were local boys who had died fighting for the Union in the Civil War.

The family's next stop was the church. The small, one-room white building sat alone in the center of the small meadow. The tended field gradually slopped down to the river where a wooden dock was now abandoned, waiting for the heat of summer to return. A well-worn dirt path meandered to the bank and what appeared like a very good fishing hole.

The church was also used as the school house. There were six long, lean windows on either side of the structure, and it was capped with a splendid steeple that housed the church bell. As the Nilssons approached, a short, chubby, balding man swooped out of the double doors. He skipped down the steps and practically danced toward the family. He quickly extended his right hand toward Hans.

"How do you do? I am Pastor Talis. So glad to see you!" Pastor Talis gave Hans's hand a few good pumps as the words tumbled out of his mouth.

"Hans. Hans Nilsson."

"Good. Good," the pastor said. His cheeks were flushed from his exuberance. "Where is the rest of your party? And Pastor Dom?" he asked as he squinted his eyes and looked over Hans's shoulder toward town.

Mary Jane stepped in after her father's imploring look. "My father is still learning English," she said with an apologetic shrug of her shoulders. "We are the first to arrive," she continued. "The rest should be here shortly, they are only a day or two behind us."

That seemed to answer the friendly pastor's questions. For his searching eyes were now filled with interest for this family who had traveled such a journey. Mary Jane introduced Bertha and the children. And after a few more minutes of her translating for her father, she was able to get directions to their farm. It was north out of town. But they would make it by nightfall. Good-byes were anything but quick. It seemed the whole town was curious about the new arrivals. But soon, they were on their way, the very last leg of the journey.

The farm was quite a distance from town. Each farm was isolated from their neighbors by miles. Traveling to town for church or for supplies would be an all day event. But the Nilssons were not disappointed. Their plot was beautiful. A creek ran through the middle of it. Hans called it Little Creek. The water spilled over gray rounded rocks. Several small pools held fish that the children squealed with delight when they spotted just under the cool water. Wild roses grew along the bank. A large bush that still held the remnants of the prolific white blooms made Bertha Nilsson stop and smile.

It was the first time Hans had seen his wife smile in many weeks.

"We shall build here, no? What a beautiful spot," she said.

Hans could not agree more. But starting that work would have to wait until tomorrow. His family had earned a good night's rest. Their first on their new land in America.

Neighbors trickled in over the next several weeks. Several wanting Hans's rock masonry expertise. He declined them all politely.

"If I do not get our house up, my baby will be born in the barn," he said with a grin. "That will not make my Bertha happy at all."

The building went fast. The barn was first. It was small with only three stalls. One for each horse, and one for the cow they were waiting for. She was coming with Pastor Dom and should arrive any day.

The cabin took longer. It was two rooms built over a small stone cellar. The rock fireplace was large and stood in the center of the cabin. A fire could be lit in the bedroom in the back simultaneously as one could be lit in the main part of the house. But Bertha would not be using this fireplace to cook on. They had purchased a new black caste iron cook stove in St. Paul. It had taken up the majority of the room in the wagon on the trip here but was worth it. And to the right of the cook stove, just next to the front door was a small four-paned glass window. A small porch was off the front door as well as the back, and right now, both doors were open to allow the evening breeze to sweep through the Nilsson home.

The scent of freshly cut lumber, pitch, and pine trees filled the home. Bertha smiled as she caressed her swollen belly. They had made it!

The last thing the stone and wooden cabin needed was a ladder to the small loft that would serve as the sleeping quarters for the children and, of course, a garden. The garden spot was selected and would be neatly arranged between the back door and the barn. It would be located close to the bank of the stream to aid in irrigation. Pine trees as well as several large chestnut and oak trees stood in the front of the home, and wild onion, lilies, and rose bushes were in the back. The homestead was beautiful. Now preparations needed to be made for the fast approaching winter.

When Pastor Dom arrived, he was shocked to see the Nilsson home nearly completed.

"You waste no time at all, Hans Nilsson," he had said as he clasped Papa affectionately on the back.

"Would you be willing to assist others with their stonework now?"

Hans knew that was coming. He was counting on it. With Bertha still so weak and their travels taking so long, they had not had anytime to store away food for the winter. They would not be able to plant a garden until spring. The Minnesota winters forbade it. Hans was counting on the extra work to either trade or purchase what his family would need.

While Hans built fireplace after fireplace for the Swedish settlers, the children gathered firewood daily. The boys, however, always found time to explore, hunt, and fish, while the girls took turns milking the cow that the family had named Ingrid.

Every night, Hans returned home with jars of green beans, beets, or fruit preserves. Slowly, the cellar was filling up with supplies. A fat deer hung off the back porch. Tonight, the family would have venison until they could eat not more. America, the land of plenty indeed!

Before the sun rose, Bertha's water broke. She did not wake Hans, for she had done this before and knew she had a few more hours before the baby would arrive. Mary Jane heard her mother bustling around below her sleeping loft. When she peered over the edge and saw Bertha gripping the back of the chair as she endured yet another contraction, Mary Jane also knew it was time for the baby. They had all been through this a few times before.

Mary Jane quickly dressed and braided her long auburn hair. Then she carefully descended the ladder to the kitchen below. Her mother rewarded her with a slight smile and a kiss on her forehead.

"I will get fresh water," Mary Jane said. Her mother only nodded as she was working through another contraction. Mary Jane grabbed the wooded bucket from the peg, just outside the back door. Her strides were long and purposeful as she made her way to the creek. Within moments, she was back in the warm kitchen, ready to set the water to boil on Mama's new cook stove. Hans was now fully awake and pulling on his coveralls. Bertha was lighting a glass lantern.

"It is time for me to lie down," Bertha said. Hans took the light from his wife and followed her into the bedroom. Bertha was correct. The baby arrived within a few hours, while Hans paced in the kitchen. All the children were wide awake by this time and anxious to meet the newest member to their family. Mary Jane was assisted by her younger sister, Nettie. Nettie was just a year younger than Mary Jane, and at fourteen, she had already helped welcome more than one baby into this world.

Little Jonathon was born in Sweden before they left. Mary Jane and Nettie had been there to help Mrs. Oslow. Mrs. Oslow had been a very experienced midwife as well as a patient and caring woman. Mary Jane's thoughts drifted back to the trip across the Atlantic and Mrs. Oslow's burial at sea. Her loss was strongly felt throughout the community, not just on this night. Eric and Alfred rode out on horseback to the closest farm where Mrs. Parson lived. She had promised to help Mama when her time came. The Parson farm was a few miles away, so it would take time for Mrs. Parson to arrive. Mama's contractions where right on top of each other now. It would not be long.

"Thank you, my girls," Bertha Nilsson said, panting. She offered a loving smile to her two daughters while she feebly squeezed Nettie's hand for reassurance.

"It won't be long now, Mama," Mary Jane said. "I can see the baby's head crowning."

Bertha Nilsson mustered up all the energy she had to give a final push. It had been a short labor, compared to the others. But Bertha was so frail, and her body was so weak. She instinctively knew this labor was much different.

"It is a boy!" Mary Jane whispered as the baby inhaled his first gulp of air and let out a feeble cry. Mary Jane fought back tears of joy, relief, and amazement. Life was such a gift.

Bertha's glazed eyes swept over her son. She smiled and kissed his small head already covered with a thick mat of dark curls.

"He looks like your father, doesn't he?" she said.

"Yes, without a moustache, of course!" Nettie replied.

Nettie rose and moved to the kitchen to make the announcement and introduction to the family. The baby was very small and quiet. Once cleaned, he was wrapped in a patchwork quilt and handed to Hans. He took the baby lovingly, kissed his forehead, then showed the precious bundle to his other children who were anxiously gathered around.

"The first American Nilsson!" Papa said with much pride. "He is beautiful."

To that, her mother smiled faintly behind closed eyelids. While the others rejoiced in the newcomer, Mary Jane stayed with her mother who was extremely weak. The bleeding had not stopped. By the time Mrs. Parson's arrived, Mary Jane had already packed her mother with ice to no avail. Mary Jane held her mother's now limp hand and wept.

Bertha was pale, and her breathing was shallow and labored. When she opened her eyes, she seemed unable to focus. Her voice no louder than a whisper.

"Mama, please," Mary Jane begged, choking on her tears.

"Mary Jane, listen to me." Mary Jane had to lean her head down near her mother's mouth to hear her faint words. "You have been a gift to me since the day you were born. I could not have asked for a better daughter. You are so strong."

Mary Jane continued to cradle her mother's hand. She wiped her own tears with the back of it and kissed it tenderly. Emotion over took her, and she could not speak. She could not even call for her father.

"Promise me," Momma continued. "Promise to take care of everyone. Be patient with the boys and…" Her voice trailed off. She was too exhausted to continue.

"I promise, Mama, I promise." Mary Jane continued to hold her mother's cool hand as she felt the life slip away. Mrs. Parson went to deliver the news to Hans. Bertha had not survived the delivery of this last Nilsson child.

Bertha Nilsson's small body barely covered the kitchen table. Mary Jane and the ladies from the church carefully cleaned her body and brushed her hair until it shone. She was dressed in her favorite dress—a blue calico with a sweet lace collar. The children gathered around the table and kissed their mother good-bye. It was a somber moment. The Nilsson children were stoic and unnaturally quiet. They looked to their father, but Hans had not said a word since Mrs. Parson's had told him his beloved Bertha had passed. He just held tightly to the baby and drank in deeply his sweet scent. A scent Bertha would never know.

They buried her in front of the large wild rose bush. In the spring, it would be covered with dainty white blossoms. Mary Jane thought of her mother smiling. She would have loved watching these flowers bloom. This thought brought her some comfort.

Comfort also came from the neighbors pouring in, their travel companions from the voyage across the Atlantic. They brought sympathetic loving words and food. Lots of food. It was a Swedish smorgasbord. Sweden's climate, location, and history are all key to the traditional cuisine. The Vikings, who inhabited all of Scandinavia thousands of years earlier, were some of the first people to develop a method for preserving food. To prepare for their long sea voyages, Viking women salted, cured, and dehydrated meat, fish, fruits, and vegetables. As these aggressive crusaders raided all across Europe, they brought back with them not only treasure, but also a variety of foods, that will be incorporated into the Swedish cuisine. These foods included fruits from the Mediterranean, sauces from France, teas from England, and sweet cakes from Germany. The word *smorgasbord* is Swedish in its origin. It is a culinary tradition. The kitchen table was heavy with the mixed aroma of dozens of different dishes from their homeland. There were warm *plattar* (Swedish pancakes with apple butter), *pepparkakor* (ginger cookies), and *lussekatter*, sweet cakes with raisins. There was *artsoppa*, a thick aromatic pea soup; *kottbulla*, Swedish meatballs; and *frestelse*, a delicious potato dish. Mourners ate and talked in quiet, dulcet tones about Hans and his eleven children. What would they do now?

The hushed conversations and consoling continued until dusk when everyone climbed into their wagons or buggies and returned to their own homes and their own happier lives. Behind, they left food that would last the family days, and twelve broken hearts that did not know what tomorrow would bring.

Remembering Sandy Lake

IT WAS OBVIOUS to the Ojibwa people that General Pope and the Great White Chief Lincoln cared nothing for the Anishinabe, the People. The people who called this land home since the beginning of time. The Old Crossing Treaty was yet another example of how Indian rights were in the way of white progress. The Ojibwa must move.

Chief Crane and the elders decided since the winter was coming fast, the best option would be to migrate to south, where the game was more plentiful. But the Minnesota Territory was now dotted with small settlements of immigrants, all staking their claim to the land. These settlements were still riveted with the tales of the Sioux and the Minnesota War and the very fresh horror of the execution of Chief Wabash and savage murder of Chief Little Crow. The people had to stay away from these white communities. To come into contact with them could prove dangerous.

There was one location that had served as a winter camp before, but it was haunted by the memories from the past. Sandy Lake.

Sandy Lake was a pristine lake that the natives had used for generations. Here, the People would fish and hunt and gather roots and berries to store for winter. They would gather materials needed to build their Birch Bark Canoes and document their history on Birch Bark Scrolls.

Sandy Lake was dotted with small islands that reminded the People of their beginnings on Turtle Island. The oral history taught the Ojibwa that seven great *miigis*—radiant magical beings came from the heavens to teach the People. One of the seven miigis was too strong and powerful. Just being in his presence was deadly to humans. He was known as the thunderbird or the powerful one. The powerful one returned to the ocean, while the other six remained and guided the Ojibwa on the path of life. Each miigis utilized an animal as his totem or symbol. One was a strong and noble *nooke* (bear). One was a patient and powerful *moozoonsii* (moose). One was an *aan'aawenh* (duck) who was comfortable on land as well as water. The fourth was a *wawaazisii* (bullhead), thoughtful and strong. And the last was the wise and knowledgeable echomaker, a *baswenaazhi* (crane). All seven beings provided gifts to the People and helped them establish the very first clans or *doodems*.

⇸ Mary Jane ⇷

The great miigis visited the chiefs in their dreams. It was in this form that the great prophecy was passed onto the People. It was said that the Ojibwa must move west to escape the white invaders. That they must migrate until they found the land with many, smaller Turtle Islands. Here they would find food that grows in water, wild rice. Here they would also find the miigis shells, cowry shells, that could be used to display their connection to the gods—the *miigis*. And so it was. Sandy Lake was one of many sacred places for the People. But just ten years earlier, the shores of Sandy Lake were stained with the blood of over four hundred of their dead.

To the Ojibwa, the land was like the air, water, or sunlight, gifts from the gods. Not something any man could own, trade, or sell. By 1850, migration to Minnesota, forced Congress to break several previous treaties and unlawfully relocate the Ojibwa people. Promised money and supplies were trapped behind political red tape. This coupled with a Minnesota harsh winter and spoiled meet from Fort Snelling caused the death of over four hundred people. Disease, starvation, and freezing temperatures took their toll. Many felt the poisoning was deliberate. The United States Government insisted it was an accident, but no compensation was ever offered.

The dead were lovingly buried in burial mounds with *jiibegamig*, or spirit houses, over each mound. Wooden markers adorned with symbols were placed at the head of each mound. These markers depicted the clan or doodem that the deceased belonged to. The banks of Sandy Lake marked this location.

The people began their march to winter camp. Their hearts were heavy with memories of the past. Once again, Chief Crane looked to the heavens for guidance. He prayed for protection from the bitter winter winds and bitter whites as well.

The Sin Eater

THE WINTER OF 1863 was yet another harsh one. Winter storms swept in from the north and raged for days. Snow piled up several feet deep, covering the steps to the front and back porch of the Nilsson cabin. The weather made hunting game more difficult for Hans Nilsson and his eldest sons—Eric who was twelve and Alfred who was eleven. Mary Jane spent most of the winter inside the warm kitchen of the log house in Minnesota. She tended the children, cooked the family's meals in the big, black cook stove, and washed and darned the clothing in this one room. Nettie helped her every step of the way. The girls together continued with the reading and writing lessons. Mary Jane's English was coming along quiet nicely. Even Hans was picking it up now. No matter how busy they kept themselves, winter provided too much quiet time for the family to reflect and remember how much they missed their mother. Her grave was covered with snow and surrounded by ice from the frozen creek. Cold and alone, how many of the Nilssons felt.

Food supplies were slim and consisted mainly of meat, deer, elk, rabbit, and even one moose that Eric was lucky enough to shoot one bitterly frigid afternoon. Ingrid, the cow, was milked daily. This was the only form of substance for the new baby that the children had named Baby Hans. The daily chores splattered with readings from the Bible or *The Odyssey* kept the family entertained. But Mary Jane craved for a childhood lost. She craved the sight of her mother, she craved friendship, socialization, and she even craved fresh fruit. She was starving for spring, and all it would bring.

The Nilssons were not the only ones suffering this winter. After Gettysburg and heavy losses at the second Bull Run, the Union forces had increased their focus on drafting able body men. Fort Snelling was the hub for new recruits. Soldiers were being dispatched daily to look for any Minnesota immigrants that had escaped the draft.

With only a few doctors in St. Paul, no schools, and the heavy snow fall keeping people from making the arduous journey to Sunday church, it was like looking for a needle in a haystack. Soldiers rode out in small battalions on horseback, trying to recruit new men to support the Northern cause to no avail.

The Chippewa had moved north of Red Lake as ordered. But the storms had pushed the wild game down south, and the Natives followed their food source. Teepees were set up in canyons that provided some shelter from the howling winds and hid them from the ever-present military scouts. It seemed every living thing was holding their breaths, patiently waiting for the reprieve that would come with the spring thaw.

A small band of Sioux dog soldiers were also in dire straights. They too were freezing and hungry. Looking for food and blankets, this small band of rouge warriors rode into the town of Brainerd. In the middle of the night, they broke into the mercantile and stole what they could easily carry. On their way out of town, they saw smoke curling from a chimney stack, a lone cabin in the woods. The warriors circled the cabin, while one peeked through the only window in the structure. When he saw a few children comfortably sitting in front of the fire, reading, they made the decision. They kicked the door in, then ransacked the cupboards, searching the small kitchen for more food, and stripped the bed of a heavy patchwork quilt.

As the children were huddled in the corner crying, the man of the house walked in from the barn. Shots were fired. It was chaos. The children screamed with terror. When the smoked cleared, one warrior lay dead as well as the man and two of his young.

"Do you know who they were?" asked Hans Nilsson.

"No," said Pastor Dom. "A Welch family, new immigrants like us all."

"The funerals will be tomorrow in town. Be aware. Be careful." With that, Pastor Dom and the men he was traveling with bundled themselves back up. They had many more houses to visit, to spread the word before night fall.

Hans closed the door behind them. He rested his head on the wood and took a deep breathe before turning to face his family.

"Off to bed with you now," he said, his voice quiet and troubled. "We will be heading to town tomorrow in the morn."

"Are we going to the funeral, Papa?" Eric asked.

"Yes, son, we are. Mary Jane, Nettie, can you—"

"Yes, Papa," Mary Jane interrupted. "We will have something baked by morning." It was, after all, a tradition—to bring food and consolation to a neighbor in need even if you did not know them well or at all.

The drive to town was long and cold. The only social this winter since Bertha's wake actually was yet another funeral. The meadow in town was full of carriages and wagons. Smoke slowly curled from the chimney in the church. The Nilssons arrived as the church bell was rung. Pastor Dom sat in the pew with his friends and neighbors, while Pastor Talis stood at the altar. His sermon was short. He spoke about life being a precious gift, and these lives cut so short. Four redheaded children sat in the front row with a redheaded woman, all weeping. The family of the three dead. One man and two boys were killed, murdered by savages.

"It's a wonder there are bodies to be buried," Eric had said.

"Yeah, I hear those savages will scalp and eat you if they have the chance," added Alfred.

"Eat you?" Nettie whimpered, obviously terrified.

Mary Jane was not sure if she believed her younger brothers' tales. But she had also heard stories of Indians.

Savages. These were the boogiemen that she had heard tales about since her youth in Sweden. She was not afraid to admit that this was what truly terrified her about the move to America. Indians. But Pastor Dom had promised that the Indian problem was under control in Minnesota. Obviously not.

When Pastor Talis was finished, he announced they would gather outside now, in the cemetery next to the church. We followed the congregation out into the day. The sun hung high in the sky. Snow covered the ground and glinted in the noon day rays. Smoke from several chimneys filled the air. It was brisk, but not uncomfortable. Mary Jane snuggled down into her cloak and wrapped the quilt more tightly around the sleeping Baby Hans who was snuggled in her arms. Nettie held the hands of the twins, George and Isaar, to keep them out of trouble. Hans was laden with three-year-old Charlie. Who could not be still or quiet? Seven-year-old Christine held baby Jonathon who was now almost two years old. The boys—Eric, Alfred, and Henry—stood next to their father. All hearts and minds were feeling a pang of their loss. Bertha had been gone only a few months, but today, it seemed like the wound was even fresher than that.

The three men were wrapped in cheese cloth, from head to toe. They were each carefully laid next to a freshly dug grave with a wooden cross baring their name at the head of each. Mary Jane looked at the deceased that she did not know. The largest cocoon was obviously the father. The two smaller ones were no larger than her. Would she have met these boys in the spring?

Would they have been classmates or even friends? She wondered as a single tear ran down her cheek and disappeared in the neck of her winter cloak.

A small parcel was unwrapped and laid atop of each body. A slice of crust bread and a hide flask full of wine for each.

"Now, turn your backs, and remember, do not look at the sin eater," said Pastor Talis.

Mary Jane looked at her father with a quizzical glance.

"Do as you are told children," Hans's voice was husky from unshed tears of his own.

The crowd turned their backs to the dead as the cemetery gate was opened. Mary Jane could hear the footsteps crunch the snow as he walked into their mist. The sin eater.

Peeking over her left shoulder, Mary Jane could make out a spirit, a monster of a man. He was covered from head to toe in a charcoal gray cloak. A hood covered his head and face.

"I give easement to these men. You will not wander forever alone, along unknown paths, for I will take on your earthly sins. I take them onto my own soul. You are now free, clean from any wrongdoing." The sin eater's voice was gruff and sent a cold shiver up Mary Jane's spine. Charlie began to weep into Papa's shoulder, obviously affected by the mans voice as well as she was.

The sin eater reached for the offering of bread and wine and gobbled them down like a starving dog. One after another. The sound was hideous. When he had consumed all three offerings, his boots again crunched the snow as he quietly left the cemetery.

Mary Jane watched in revulsion as he seemed to almost float away from the meadow and disappear into the pine tree forest beyond. What had she just experienced?

The ride home went more quickly that the ride to town in the morning. Hans was eager to get home and finish his chores before sundown. He was also eager to get away from his children and their unending questions about today's event and the sin eater. He had been shocked himself and had asked only a few questions to gain some insight. He shared what he knew with his curious clan.

"Apparently, it is an old Welsh custom," he began when they were well on their way down the quiet road home. "The sin eater was selected from their group that immigrated here before we arrived. They leave food and drink as tokens, gifts for the poor man. Then he takes the tokens, taking on their sin…so their souls can move on with out regret, I suppose."

"Why would anyone want to take on another man's sins?" asked Alfred, always the scholar.

"I am not sure, son," replied Hans. "I guess because it is important to their people. Maybe he thinks it is his duty, his job. They believe in it enough, that they still practice it."

"Do we need a sin eater?" asked Eric quietly.

"Absolutely not, Eric. What sin have you committed besides eating too much?" Hans had hoped a little levity would end the excruciating conversation. It did not.

"What sins did those boys commit?" asked Eric, still perplexed.

"None, I am sure," stated Hans without hesitation.

"Perhaps it was just their violent deaths. Those poor boys suffered. I do not know. Every one handles grief very differently." Hans knew this only too well.

"How was that man selected for this job, Papa?" Nettie asked next.

"I was told by Pastor Dom that they drew lots. Each man put his mark on something, and whoever's was drawn got the horrible task of being the community's sin eater," Hans replied.

"Was he a monster, Papa?" asked Nettie again.

"No, Nettie. Just a man," Hans Nilsson answered stoically. Sadness was thick in his voice.

Mary Jane sighed. "A sad man."

"Imagine," she continued, "no one touching you or looking at you or loving you. Ever. They turned their backs on him, while he took on their sins! That was a sad man, I think." Mary Jane could not keep the tears at bay now.

Hans placed his arm around his daughter's shoulders and drew her near. She rested her head on her father's strong arm and openly wept. She wept for the loss of her mother, for them all, and for how their lives had changed. And she wept for the sin eater as well.

"I think you are right, bobbin," Hans said. "He must be a sad mad indeed."

Hans felt some of his own grief wafting away. The loss of Bertha was heavy on his heart. But he had a wagon full of loving, caring children that he could touch and look at anytime he wanted comfort or companionship. He was a wealthy man to be sure to have so much. He wiped away a tear and squeezed Mary Jane even tighter to his side. Yes, he was a wealthy man indeed.

Wendigo

"FIRST, YOU WOULD smell him." Nooka crouched around the fire retelling the story for the hundredth time. He had the children riveted. He raised his hands in front of his chest and using the glow of the firelight he turned his fingers into horrific claws as he continued.

"The smell of rotting flesh, decay, and death!" He lunged forward and was rewarded with the squeals from his entranced audience.

Nooka (Tender Bear) was the clan's young medicine man. He still had much to learn, so was also given the task of regularly sharing the history of the clan with the children. Time at winter camp was often spent story telling. A job he thoroughly enjoyed.

"His gray skin is hairless and pulled tightly over his bones. His eyes are yellow and sunken into his skull. He looks like a walking skeleton." Nooka paused here for dramatic effect. Some of the children where hiding behind their knees pulled up tightly to their chest, while others eagerly leaned forward awaiting the next ghastly detail.

"His mouth! His mouth!" a few cried out.

Nooka took the suggestion and continued. "His mouth? His lips looked like flesh falling from bone. Covered in blood but not his own. It is the blood of his last victim."

The Wendigo. Not just a story to the Ojibwa. For generations, the stories were told and retold of the mystical monster that was once a human being. A cannibalistic creature that did the unthinkable. When winter caused men to go hungry, the story was told to remind the People to walk the path of the spirits. Once you tasted human flesh, you could never go back. You were lost and could be transformed into the monster—the Wendigo.

"The Wendigo can never eat enough. After consuming one victim, he must begin the search for his next," Nooka continued.

The Wendigo had become a part of the People's culture. More than just a story. A reminder that gluttony and greed would take even a holy man down the wrong path. Excess was not a part of the life of the Ojibwa. These were people who shared everything—their supplies, their work, their celebrations, and their mourning. The entire tribe was built around the concept of cooperation and caring for Mother Mature and her many gifts. This included their fellow man.

"The Wendigo are like the white men!" one young boy cried out. This was a comparison they had all heard many times before.

"They are never satisfied!" the young, some day a warrior, exclaimed.

"And they smell bad too!" added another young and eager voice. He was rewarded with a round of laughter.

In times of famine, the Ojibwa would often perform the *wiindigookaanzhimowin*, a ceremonial dance to reinforce the taboo of cannibalism. The dancer wore a mask of the hideous monster. He was believed to be many times larger and much stronger than a human man. He danced backward to the drum, symbolizing that this was the wrong direction, a different path that the one chosen by the People.

The Draft

SPRING FINALLY ARRIVED, though slower than the Nilsson family had hoped. When the snow finally left the field and green grass began to poke its shy head above the rich Minnesota soil, life again flowed into their veins.

The children spent as much time as they could outside, again exploring. Laughter echoed off the hills and filled the small log cabin. The stream began to bubble and gurgled along, and again fish and wild life could easily be spotted. Several trees began to leaf out, and the wild rose bush sent up new sprouts, as if it instinctively new that all were watching and hoping for a beautiful show above Bertha Nilsson's grave.

The boys continued to hunt with Hans, while the girls took care of the younger children. Cooking and cleaning were time consuming, but neither Mary Jane nor Nettie ever let their father hear them complain. Hans himself felt alive again. He would, however, not be able to sleep through the night until the garden was planted. He was unsure how they had survived such a long and harsh winter with so few food storages. He would not let that happen again.

Ingrid the cow was fat and happy as well, with fresh spring grass to eat. Her milk was thicker than ever. This made Baby Hans plump up, but he was still not taking too well to solid foods.

The Minnesota soil was as rich as they had dreamed. As the till dug into the earth, dark brown soil was turned much to the delight of all. Seeds of potatoes, beans, beets, corn, onion, squash, and a variety of other vegetables were planted in the yard. When this was completed, Hans and his boys began to plant eighty acres of hay. They were also going to plant corn in the north field. It seemed that life in America was finally progressing along smoothly.

This evening, Hans was on the roof of the cabin, repairing a few loose shingles. He saw the dust cloud first. A dust cloud made from hundreds of hoofs. Within moments, the boys ran to the home from the field, alarmed as the cloud came closer to the Nilsson cabin. As the cloud followed the bend in the road, Hans became alarmed. It was obviously not a storm or a stampede. Mary Jane came out the front door to verify what she had seen from the small kitchen window. Within moments, alarm turned to sheer terror.

"To the cellar boys, quickly. You must hide yourselves," Hans commanded.

The eldest Nilsson boys, Eric and Alfred, rushed past Mary Jane to climb into the cellar as their father had demanded. The cellar door was in the center of the kitchen, hidden under a rag rug. The kitchen table sat on top of that. Hiding the cellar completely from those who did not know its existence.

"What is it, Papa?" Mary Jane could hardly breathe.

"Mary Jane, be calm," Hans stated as he slowly climbed off the roof and stood on the front porch beside her. Nettie came onto the porch to join them, trying to catch her breath at moving the kitchen table alone and rapidly. The three of them stood silently, each taking deep calming breaths. The tension was thick between them.

"Girls, you must do something for me. Do not tell anyone about Eric and Al."

There was no time for any more questions. The dust cloud was upon them. Hans was right. It was a direct result of hundreds of hooves—120 hooves, to be exact. Thirty horses carried thirty Union soldiers right to the Nilssons front porch. Their blue uniforms were covered with dust. Mary Jane could see the dirt and sweat on each man's face and neck. They looked tired and irritable from days of riding.

Every soldier was also decorated with a variety of weapons. Each man carried a hand gun at his waist, several men also had riffles and two of them had swords hanging from their hips.

"Good day, sir," said the blond man in front. "I am Lieutenant Chambers. I represent General Pope and the Missouri Militia out of Fort Snelling. What is your name?"

"I am Hans Nilsson," he calmly said as he stepped off the porch and stood in front of the men on horse back. He looked small but very brave and in control of his emotions.

The lieutenant could hear Hans struggle with his broken English. It was obvious he was one of the newer immigrants to this area. A man who had thus far escaped the draft and his duty to his new country. This disgusted the lieutenant. He had lost a brother at Gettysburg and his best friend Alfred had died at Bull Run. These immigrants wanted to live here—wanted to be Americans—but were not willing to aid in the nation's survival. Disgust was carried through his voice as he spoke.

"Well, Hans Nilsson, as I am sure you are aware, every Minnesota citizen has an obligation to the United States Government and the Union army." He continued to recite a statute that he had obviously recited several times.

A citizen was a white male over eighteen years old. It will not be until after the Civil War with the passing of the Fourteenth Amendment in 1866, that black men will be considered citizens. The Fifteenth Amendment will then give black men the right to vote. Women, however, will not be considered citizens and therefore will not have the right to vote in the United States until 1919 when Congress passes the Nineteenth Amendment.

Hans knew where this was going. He was being drafted by the Union army. He had been aware that this was a possibility since his family fled the New York City Harbor last year. Now his only concern was to keep these men from taking Eric and Alfred as well.

They were so young, and Mary Jane would need their hunting skills in order to survive. Many young men under the age of eighteen were fighting in the Civil War. Some were drafted as drummers, ditch diggers, and messengers. But Lincoln was desperate for soldiers. Countless boys where taken from their homes to fight for the cause. Many were much younger that eighteen years. Military leaders would ask young boys, "Are you over eighteen?"

Patriotic young men looking for action on the battlefield found a way around this. On a shard of parchment, they would right the number 18, then place it in their shoe. This allowed them to answer the questions honestly. Yes, they were indeed *over* 18. Because the need for fresh soldiers was so great, little more attentions was paid to the age question.

"You must come with us," Lieutenant Chambers said, exhaustion evident in his voice and across his brow.

Papa silently nodded his head. He would go quickly and without protest. This would ensure that the boys would not be found in their hiding place.

The good-byes were excruciating. Mary Jane and Nettie dissolved into tears. They pleaded with the lieutenant to leave their father to no avail. Hans simply squared his shoulders, grasped, and kissed each of his daughters on their foreheads and whispered in their ears.

"Be strong, girls," he began, barely able to hold back his own tears. "Take care of each other and your little brothers and sisters." Now the tears were clearly falling from them all. "I am so proud of you both," he continued.

"Come back to us, Papa." Mary Jane pleaded. Hans simply nodded his head. But that was not enough for Mary Jane. "Come back to us, Papa! Promise me!" Her voice full of urgency.

"I will come back, I promise," he said. His voice was husky with emotion.

Hans swung his leg over the rear of a spotted Appaloosa. He sat behind a soldier who looked to be the same age as Mary Jane. As the horse turned to follow the others, Hans looked over at shoulder at his two daughters weeping on the front porch of his cabin.

He thought to himself, *Is this the American dream?*

He was off to fight a war he knew nothing about. Leaving behind eleven parentless children. It was difficult to believe that coming to America was the best thing for his family.

It was difficult indeed.

The Sweat Lodge

SPIRITUAL BELIEFS AND rituals were the heart of the Chippewa way of life. Spirits guided them through their lives. Spirit guardians visited in visions and dreams. The Sweat Lodge was the building crucial for communicating with this mystical realm.

Building the Sweat Lodge was a spiritual task of its own. The lodge was built with great care from the sacred materials used and its location. A fire pit was built away from where construction began. Carefully selected stones gathered from the banks of the river were placed in the pit in order to heat thoroughly. Once the fire was roaring and the supplies were ready, the drum began. The beat was ancient. Sacred. Powerful. It signaled the spirits that the People were preparing. Preparing to honor them. Preparing to connect with them, yet again.

The door would face the fire that was now blazing. Several tribesmen gathered around in reverent silence, simply to watch. The builders had fasted the last two days in preparation. Everything was in place.

First, the framework went up. Birch saplings specifically selected for the lodge, were stripped. They were woven together to produce an oblong-shaped dwelling. Once the framework was in place, the birch bark mats were carefully placed as the outer layer of the lodge. The four sacred directions were located and marked with totems, emblems to honor the sacred space.

The Chippewa viewed the world in two genders, animate and inanimate, rather than male and female. As an animate, each person within the tribe would serve the society in whatever way best utilized their skills. Each band had their own council, with leaders to protect and guide their community. Some of these leaders were male, some female. Several leaders from other bands would be joining them at the lodge this ceremony. Questions needs to be asked, and answers, discussed.

The question that plagued the People this season was where to go. Since the last treaty, it was demanded that the Chippewa people move from their home. Migrating to other camps was getting more challenging as white settlements spread across the landscape. Scouts were still vigilant and kept the People out of the sights of the military in blue. But lately, the white man's war was affecting the People more and more.

The Chippewa documented their history on birch bark scrolls using a written language that was unique like the People themselves. These scrolls were read and reread in order to teach and remember. Several would be examined to fully understand what the demands were on the tribe. And they must act fast. Minnesota winters were always just around the bend.

Charlie

FOR DAYS, THE Nilsson children sat, dazed and confused. Mary Jane knew without doubt that she must be the one to encourage her brothers and sisters to continue. They needed to take care of the crops and tend the garden. They needed to gather and collect whatever berries and fruit they could find and can what they could to prepare for winter. That is what summer was for, to prepare for winter.

The children dug a small canal from the garden to Little Creek. Ice was still clogging areas of the creek in the shade and shadows. But when the ice sheets were broken, and later in the summer, when the ice was gone, this would provide good water flow to the vegetables they planted here.

"What's this, Mary Jane?" asked little Charlie.

Charlie recently turned five years old. His birthday came and went without much fanfare. With Papa leaving, none of the children felt much like celebrating, and Mary Jane forgot. For this, she would always feel guilt.

"Corn," she answered him as she weeded.

"Oh." His puckered lips were absolutely adorable. So were his chubby little cheeks as they slowly took on a red tint in the sunshine. Charlie had dirty blond hair that curled uncontrollably. His curls were large enough for Mary Jane to stick her finger through them. One curl covered his left eye, while another one tickled his ear. A plump, dirty hand swatted at the ticklish ear without much luck. That curl had a mind of its own.

"What's this, Mary Jane?" he asked as he stepped on two tender plants just breaking through the soil.

"That is squash. Be careful," she snapped.

With that, a little pink nose splattered with freckles wrinkled up distorting the adorable face.

"Ugh, why did you plant squash? I don't like squash!" he said with disgust.

"I know Charlie does not like squash, but George and Isaar like squash," she answered with a smile.

"Let them eat it," he said as he happily picked up a worm and juggled it from one dirty hand to another.

"What's this, Mary Jane?" came yet another question. Would they ever end?

"Pumpkins," she said, almost exasperated. Charlie asked a lot of questions often. Why is the sky blue? Why is fire hot? How do birds fly? Why can't I go fishing too? Why do I have to take a bath? When will Papa be home? Some questions were harder to answer than others.

"Will we carve pumpkins, Mary Jane? Charlie will make a Jack-o'-Lantern!" He squealed as he dropped his worm. He scrambled in the dirt, looking for his squirmy treasure.

"Yes," she said. "Charlie will make a Jack-o'-lantern."

"Oooooh," he said, very pleased. A smile spread across his face.

"Good, Papa will like that." Mary Jane watched his little body trip to the creek where his older brothers were fishing. "Be careful of the ice," Mary Jane called.

Evenings were the hardest. Getting every one fed, clean, and in bed was often exhausting. But evenings also held some of Mary Jane's favorite moments. Reading the adventures from *The Odyssey* to her siblings was rewarding. Nettie often read as well, but tonight, she rocked Baby Hans as Mary Jane read aloud.

Tonight's story was about the hero Odysseus and his men. They landed on yet another strange island in the Aegean Sea. On this island, the men were captured by a giant one eyed monster called a Cyclops. Odysseus once again would use his brain to design a cleaver escape. He and his men shared wine with the giant while trapped in a cave along with several sheep. When the Cyclops finally fell into a drunken slumber, Odysseus blinded the monster with a spear to his only eye. The monster awoke in a terrible rage.

This had the Nilsson children leaning forward, gripping onto every word out of Mary Jane's mouth.

"Use the scary voice Mary Jane!" Charlie urged.

Aiming to please her audience, Mary Jane, in a deep, raspy voice, read for the giant. As the monster felt the top of each of his beloved sheep, he let them out of the cave and to safety. His hopes were to trap Odysseus and his men with in the dark confines for his ultimate punishment. But Odysseus again proved his superior intelligence. He and his men hung onto the bellies of the sheep and were able to sneak out of the cave, right under the giant's nose. This thrilled the children. The boys loved the battles, while the girls loved the mythology. But they all felt Odysseus was the bravest man ever, second only to their Papa.

In the morning, the children all walked along the creek. The ice was thick in some areas, still thick enough to walk on. They were looking for a good spot to fish. It had been a while since the family had had fresh meat, and the past few hunting trips had been unsuccessful for Eric and Alfred.

"Odysseus woulda caught a deer," Charlie chided.

"You don't catch a deer, Charlie," Henry sneered.

"You shoot a deer," Alfred added.

"Well, Odysseus woulda got one. Maybe two," he said, smug in his knowledge of his mythic hero.

They continued to walk the slippery bank. Charlie was instantly bored and started to throw rocks. He liked the way they bounced off the ice and skidded to the other side of the creek, like a discus that Odysseus himself had thrown at one of the great monster he battled. Down further, the ice was almost completely gone, and the water meandered into a small meadow. But the children were quite a distance from the meadow as of yet.

Mary Jane was distracted from Charlie and his Olympic rock tossing when Christine spotted a young deer in the clearing. The older boys sprinted to the cabin to retrieve the rifle. Perhaps they would have fresh meet tonight after all.

It only took a moment.

One moment, and he was gone. There was not even much of a splash.

Charlie had fallen in the creek. Mary Jane rushed to the frozen bank while panic filled her. Little Charlie was trapped under the ice. His cherub face looking up at her through the cloudy barrier.

Mary Jane beet and clawed at the ice like a frantic animal. A guttural cry for help escaped her mouth, alerting the other children to the danger.

Within moments, several Nilsson children frantically clawed at the ice alongside Mary Jane. Rocks were used to smash the surface to no avail. They were in a shady spot. Here the ice was still too thick. The current swept Charlie down stream as the children ran and cried at the horror that was taking place in front of their eyes.

Mary Jane watched his little face, just below the surface, only inches from her now raw and bloody fingertips. She saw the moment water entered his lungs. He coughed frantically. And then, his eyes fluttered for the last time.

Mary Jane watched as the life slipped from her little brother.

At the meadow, where the ice was thin, the children were finally able to remove Charlie from Little Creek. His wet curls stuck to his cold neck and face. His long, thick eyelashes lay still on his chubby cheeks. His voice was silent. There would be no more questions, no Jack-o'-Lantern, no more Odysseus trivia.

His light was gone.

They buried Charlie next to his mother. Under the wild rose bush on the banks of the stream that took his life.

Turn of the Seasons

FOR THE OJIBWA, the changing of the seasons was a demonstration of the power of the spirit gods. The primary essence of the People was unity, oneness with all living things. In order for life to continue in harmony, there must be birth, growth, death, and then new birth or renewal. This was spring. Renewal.

The People knew this. They felt it in their heart and soul. It was taught to them in songs and stories, in dances and ceremonies. Songs were sung to them by their grandmothers around the fire. *Nokomis*, grandmothers. The storytellers.

The People knew the prophecy. It was shared with them by the seven great miigis, the radiant spirit gods that visited the People in the beginning. Europeans would overtake the Ojibwa with their overwhelming power and sheer numbers. It was because of this prophecy that the People left their original home on Turtle Island by the ocean and moved west to the Great Lake

Region. Now here, their former domain was teeming with towns and flooded with white settlers.

The Ojibwa, or Chippewa as they were more commonly known, were semi-nomadic people from the beginning. In the summer months, families returned to their gardens and camped on the banks of cool water ways. Here, they gathered birch bark for canoes, scrolls, and storage containers. They fished, hunted, and gathered berries and roots to be used as medicines. They were often joined by other bands and had time for feasts and ceremonies including the sun dance.

In the fall, it was time to move camp to where the wild rice grew. Bands separated to begin the vital task of harvesting, parching, and jigging the rice. The dried grain was then carefully stored in pitch lined birch bark containers, ready for winter. The People relished in the color changes of the trees. As their world turned from green to orange, they knew it was time to migrate to their next camp.

Winter camps were nestled in the forests, among the red and white pines. Here they were protected from the fierce winter winds and their wigwams were easily hidden in the brush. Winter was the time for storytelling, crafts, fishing though the ice, and trapping. The profitable fur trade with their French friends to the north enabled the People to sustain their standard of living. But after the war between the States began, French exploration declined. The People felt the loss of this income coupled with promised annual payments of food and supplies from the American government being scarce, winter soon became known as the dying time for the People.

But spring was a promise of new life.

Spring camps were among the maple trees and sugar bushes. The People rejoiced in gathering the tree sap, boiling it down in a sweet syrup and then dried sugar. This was a task the women and children had done for generations. And it gave the People a sense of normalcy. All was right with the world, if only temporarily.

As the ice began to break away from the stream beds, the men in the village began their spear fishing. Fresh fish was yet another reminder of the splendors of spring. Several young men walked along the banks for hours, until the stream opened into a small sun filled meadow. Here, the ice was cleared, and the fish were biting. After a quick meal of the day's catch, a short nap in the sunshine was in order before the long hike back to the village.

The men were awoken by screams and shouts. They sprang into motion, weapons at the ready. In crouched positions, they carefully maneuvered themselves through the grass for a closer look. Several pale-faced children where gathered around the stream, intently examining whatever was just under the ice. As they frantically entered the small meadow, completely unaware of the Ojibwa hunters, one girl plunged into the cool water. She climbed out on the opposite bank, losing her footing more than once, unable to use her arms to assist her climb up the muddy slope. Her arms were full. She cradled the body of child. A child that had passed to the spirit world.

Anne Marie Fritz

The young Ojibwa hunters quietly slipped from the brush and disappeared into the woods. None of them spoke, lost in their own thoughts. It was not only the Ojibwa people that had seen their share of death this season.

The War between the States

HANS HAD TRAVELED for weeks with the First Minnesota Regiment. President Lincoln had called for three hundred thousand troops and Minnesota Governor Alexander Ramsey intended to provide as many fresh soldiers from the Empire State as possible. Fort Snelling was utilized as the training center and hub for all military campaigning in the area.

The First Minnesota Regiment had already made a name for themselves. They had arrived on the Gettysburg Battlefield, day two of the campaign. It was July 2, 1863. Due to their numbers, solid training, and ambition to make a name for themselves, they took the field at Cemetery Ridge, and the battle turned in favor of the Union. By the sunset on July 3, thanks in large to those brave Minnesota boys, the north was the clear victor.

Over four thousand Swedish immigrants were or had been enlisted with the First Minnesota Regiment. Hans found this to be a great help in strengthening his English skills, also his ties to America and understanding the purpose of the Civil War. Sweden had been opposed to slavery for generations. Hans Nilsson was no different. If America was truly to be the land of opportunity, it needed to provide this opportunity to all of its inhabitants, black and white.

Drills, marching, then more drills kept him busy and exhausted. He found little time during the day to worry about his children or mourn the loss of his wife. But in the evening, it was a different story. There was too much quiet. He missed the sound of Mary Jane's voice as she read from *The Odyssey*. He missed the constant pranks of the twins, Isaar and George. He missed walking in the woods, hunting alongside Alfred and Eric. He missed the prattling questions from ever curious little Charlie. And he missed the sweetness of his eldest daughters, their kind words and thoughtfulness, and watching them love the babies. He often thought what wonderful adults they would all be, if they can survive. Life in America was difficult, and he prayed they would all see each other once again. Hans Nilsson was not convinced he would be able to keep his promise to Mary Jane.

"Come back to us, Papa. Come back to us, promise me," she had begged him with tears in her eyes.

He had made that promise, and he was going to do everything he could to keep his word.

✤ Mary Jane ✤

The early morning of May 4, 1864, the mist hung along the valley floor. The First Minnesota Regiment was camped along the banks of the Rappahannock River, Virginia.

Spring runoff caused the river to run swift and unpredictable. This morning, the camp was unnervingly quiet. The men had received their orders the night before. Today, they would march into battle.

Ulysses S. Grant had been promoted to lieutenant general over a month ago. This gave Grant command of all the land forces in the United States. His main objective was to use all the considerable might of the Union forces, in a carefully planned, well-orchestrated campaign, to crush the rebellion once and for all! The last bloody chapter had begun. It was decided that by hammering the enemy continuously. Their resources would soon dwindle, and the rebels would have no choice but to surrender.

There were two major Confederate armies in the field: General Joseph E. Johnson in Tennessee and General Robert E. Lee himself in northern Virginia. Grant planned to attack simultaneously.

Union Major General William Tecumseh Sherman, and his men were positioned and ready to attack Johnston, down south, while Major General George G. Meade's army was protecting the line along the Potomac River and Washington, DC, beyond. This would leave Grant and his army in a prime location to push General Lee and his rebels south and take the Confederate capital of Richmond, Virginia.

West of Chancellorsville, Virginia, the troops marched across swollen rivers and through miles of jungle like forests. Forests consisting of second-growth timber, thick and tangled underbrush and debris. The terrain was ragged and treacherous. Artillery and cavalry would be virtually useless in this wilderness. As they crossed the Rapidan River, the scattering of bleached bones served as a grisly reminder of an unsuccessful battle in these same woods a year earlier. Grant pushed his men on.

In the early morning of May 5, the brush gave way to plowed fields. The community of Chancellorsville was only miles away. But the Confederates were ready. A ferocious clash was initiated by Lee's men, who felt duty bound to protect this last line of defense between the Union troops and their own capital city. As the sun set over the blood-soaked battlefield that first night, it appeared that the Confederates would be victorious.

Lee's right-hand man, Confederate Lieutenant General Longstreet was seriously wounded by friendly fire and needed to be replaced. This caused the South to lose crucial momentum. By mid-afternoon on May 6, Union reserves arrived, and Grant and his army were able to storm the wooden barricades and successfully take the field. Tinder dry barricades were set ablaze. As the fire engulfed the desiccated kindling, smoke filled the air, causing more confusion and providing valuable cover as the Union forces prepared for their final advancement.

Sparks were caught in a western breeze, landing on rebel artillery. Explosions rocked the earth. Within an hour, Union troops drove the rebels back, and the Battle at Fort Wilderness was over. Due to the rough terrain and the sprawling location of the battlefield, casualty numbers were nearly impossible to compile. The Confederate's claimed they had over eight thousand men either dead or missing. The Union troops claimed they had over two thousand killed and over three thousand missing. Many were from the First Minnesota Regiment.

The rebels had not been able to stop Grant from continuing his advance on Richmond, Virginia. They would, however, have another chance at Spotsylvania, Virginia, only a few short miles to the south. Grant would be there for the battle on May 8 as would Hans Nilsson. Hans had survived this hellish ordeal. He had survived his first Civil War battle. He did have a promise to keep after all.

The Intruder

THE SUMMER QUICKLY became dreadfully hot. Keeping the garden and the fields irrigated was a daunting task for the Nilsson children. The first week of July 1864 saw some strange occurrences in Minnesota. A drought caught the farmers by surprise. The heat wave lasted for weeks on end. Water evaporated, leaving creek beds dry as bones. Little Creek that was once a frozen death trap was now nothing but a warm, muddy trickle.

The hay and corn crops were long abandoned. Now the children focused all their attention on keeping the garden alive. This was their food source for the following winter. Mary Jane and Nettie canned what they could and dried any extra meat when the boys were successful. But the family ate up their surplus as fast as they set it in storage.

The final blow to the Midwest came in mid-July, and it was biblical. A swarm of locusts ate the majority of the crops in the area. The only way the farmers had to beat the invasion was to burn them out. Smoke filled the air for days, and when it cleared, it appeared that the wrath of God had let his vengeance loose on the citizens of Minnesota.

Nary a field survived, either decimated by insects or fire. The heat wave continued as did the drought. When there was nothing left to eat, the locust move on to literally greener pastures. The Nilsson children did what they could. When Ingrid the cow died, it was almost more than Mary Jane could take. Now she had nothing to feed her siblings and no milk for the baby. Late that night, the boys butchered Ingrid. She was mostly skin and bones, but what little meat they could glean from her carcass would feed the family who had loved her like a pet.

Days dragged on. The children became weaker from lack of nutrition and lack of fresh clean water. The boys had given up hunting near the homestead. It was obvious that even the wildlife had relocated to a less hostile environment. Mary Jane awoke one morning and realized she was about to fry up the last of the meat. After this meal, there would be nothing.

She pulled out the cast-iron frying pan and felt her heart drop with despair. She had promised Papa she would take care of her little brothers and sisters. And look how that had turned out. How many graves would Papa find when he finally came home?

It took a moment for the sound to register. Mary Jane stopped her melancholy wondering when she recognized it to be footsteps she heard. Footsteps! Someone was on the front porch. Nettie rushed to peer out the small glass window with Mary Jane right behind her.

What the girls saw made their blood run cold.

Spinning sharply on her heel, Mary Jane turned to her siblings and quietly whispered the command, "Hide!"

Children scattered, some slipping under the bed, some behind the wood box. Every one held their breaths.

The pound on the door was loud and caused the Nilsson children to jump. Mary Jane's heart was in her throat, and she found her mouth instantly so parched it hurt.

Another pound on the front door.

Then another.

Mary Jane froze where she was. Her knees locked, and she found it difficult to think.

Then the door swung open.

Her time to plan had passed. The light from outside burst into the small dark cabin. It splashed across the wooden floor. Sunlight, usually so welcome now was blinding and terrifying. In the doorway was the perfect silhouette of a giant man. An Indian man.

He was so large that his body filled the door jam. Mary Jane had to tell herself not to faint. Slowly, the monster of a man ducked his head and took one long, purposeful stride inside the cabin. He was only feet away from Mary Jane.

Her heart was pounding in her ears. Her hands began to sweat. She slowly swallowed as she took a sweeping glance over the intruder. He stood taller than any man she had ever seen. Muscles rippled just under his tawny skin. He was bare-chested, save for a necklace of bear claws that encircled his tree trunk–sized neck. He wore buckskin pants with a beaded apron that was tied around his trim waist. His dark hair hung straight down his back in two long braids that were tied at the end with strips of raw hide. His feet were adorned with moccasins that had a puckered, bead work of red and blue across the top.

But truly what made Mary Jane's breath catch was his face. Steely black eyes looked down a sharp nose at her as he towered above. High cheekbones punctuated the red painted hand print that covered his mouth and jaw.

He was terrifying.

Mary Jane stood frozen. Her heart beat was deafening. Could he hear it too?

She knew immediately her brothers were correct. This man was the monster they had been warned of. He was going to eat them. He was the boogieman indeed.

"*Peonagowink kino waiba.*" His deep voice shattered the tense silence in the room as it washed over them.

The cast-iron skillet felt heavy in her right hand. It would have to do. She pulled the pan off the stove, its contents scattered across the cabin floor behind her. Holding the pan with both hands now over head, she gritted through her teeth.

"If you want my brothers and sisters, you will have to get past me first!"

Her arms strained with the weight of her weapon, but her will was stronger. She would not allow another member of her family to die.

→ MARY JANE ←

The man looked at her soberly. His eyes were dark and held no clues as to what he was thinking or planning. A shiver ran up Mary Jane's spine. She felt the full gravity of the situation and never missed her father more.

Without a word, he took a single long step around her. His steely eyes combed the interior of their home. The place that once felt so safe and full of love. Now it felt cold and small like a confining cell. He walked around the now very cramped kitchen and pointed at each of the Nilsson children in their hiding place.

As he found them, he spoke. His voice was quiet, but powerful. The children were frozen with terror.

He pointed at Nettie behind the door. "*Bezhig.*"

He pointed at Alfred under the bed. "*Niizh.*"

Then he pointed at Henry who was also under the bed. "*Niswi.*"

He pointed at George and Isaar in the wood box. "*Niiwin ye Naanan.*"

Oh my Lord, Mary Jane thought with horror. He was counting them!

He took another step and turned his body until his eyes met Eric's. "*Ingodwaaswi.*" Six.

Christine was "*niizhwaaswi.*" Seven. Christine was silently crying as she clung to Jonathon.

Jon was "*ishwaaswi.*" Eight.

The giant Indian then stepped next to the cradle where Baby Hans lay. Hans had not had milk for days. He had long since stopped crying from sheer exhaustion. Mary Jane knew his little life was hanging by a thread.

As the massive Indian peered into the crib, a sound escaped his lips that sounded like disgust. Then quietly, more quiet than the others, he said, "*Zhaangaswi.*" Nine.

He took another step this time back toward the doorway. He turned and looked directly into Mary Jane's eyes. "*Midaaswi,*" he said.

Yes, she was number ten.

With that, he walked out the door.

For a moment, the cabin was silent. Shock was heavy in the air. Then the little ones' weeping broke the silence.

Mary Jane knew she had no choice. They had no choice. They must make the arduous walk to the nearest neighbor's homestead. It was miles away, but they had no choice. They could not wait here for the savages to return for them. That was a chance she could not take. Many of the Nilsson children were too weak for such a journey. They still had the wagon, but without sturdy horses, it was useless.

Mary Jane rushed to the garden spot and dug in the dry earth with her bare hands. She was looking for anything they could eat. Anything. A few wild onions was all she was able to collect. The heat of the day was stiffening already.

"Okay," she said, panting. Her mind was racing, deciding her best route to safety.

"Everyone down in the cellar. We will wait until this evening. It will be cooler and make it easier for us travel," she said.

"It will make it easier for us to hide too," added Eric somberly.

Mary Jane had been thinking the same thing, but it seemed too frightening to say it aloud. Eric's words hung in the air. Full confirmation that she was not the only one who knew the severity of their situation.

The cellar was dark and cool. The earthy smell, momentarily comforting. Mary Jane sat directly on the dirt floor and put her back against the cool, sturdy rock wall her father's hands had built himself. She remembered collecting these rocks, one at a time from the creek bed, her and her siblings, and Mama.

That had been a happier time.

They were all so excited to finally be here in Minnesota. So excited for their new life. Who could have foreseen how it would have all played out? Had they known how grueling cutting out a life in the wilderness would be, would they have come at all? Would they have left Sweden?

Her wandering came to an abrupt halt when George sat in her lap. The other children were gathered around her as close as they could. All of them touching, hugging, comforting. As her eyes adjusted to the dark, she could make out the tiny faces of her little brothers, usually so brave and tough, now scared and uncertain. Her sisters were weak and tired, hungry, and terrified. They all looked to Mary Jane for strength and guidance. She inhaled deeply, smelling the odor of the cellar mixed with the little boy who was now cradled in her arms.

"We will be okay," she said, steadier this time. Her voice concealed her true feelings of dread. "We will leave as soon as it turns dark. You will see, everything will be all right."

The children rested without talking. Each of them privately preparing for their escape. Baby Hans whimpered. Without milk, soon he would surely perish. It would be a long night but a necessary one. Mary Jane knew she had to stay strong, stay focused, and get her family to safety. Six-year-old George placed a small, warm hand on her cheek. That was all the incentive she needed.

Spotsylvania

AFTER THE DEVASTATION at Wilderness Campaign just two days earlier, General Grant had a plan. A counterattack. He planned to keep the rebels on the run, and what better way to do that than to strike while the iron was hot.

The night of May 7, 1864, Grant ordered his men to march southeast to the Spotsylvania Court House. Spotsylvania was a strategic location. It served as the cross roads that controlled all trade routes from the southern states directly to the Confederate capital of Richmond, Virginia. Richmond was more than just the rebel's capital—it was their stronghold. Grant was determined to position his forces between the Confederates and their beloved capital city. This was the only way to force the Confederate troops to fight out in the open, not among the trees like the brutal Wilderness Campaign.

The wagons were heavily burdened with artillery. This coupled with exhausted men made for slow traveling. The wagons kicked up a dust cloud that hung in the air as heavy as the men's hearts. The Wilderness Campaign was still fresh on their clothes and in their minds. Friends hastily buried and so many of them. The deadly assault had reached a fever pitch that many had never seen the like. And all dreaded seeing again.

"The Confederates fought like the devil himself." This was a sentiment repeated with disbelief. They silently prayed that Spotsylvania would be much different.

The Confederate General Robert E. Lee was proud of the strength and bravery his men had displayed. But when he saw the dust cloud hanging in the stagnate air, he knew it was Grant and his men repositioning themselves for another rally. What was in that direction? Of course, the crossroads of Spotsylvania. If the Union troops took Spotsylvania, it was a clear march to the Confederate capital, Richmond.

Knowing the terrain had been beneficial to the Confederate troops several times throughout the war. Lee and his men would take to the forest, avoiding the road. They would take every back trail they knew to beat Grant and his men. As darkness fell, the Confederate troops lit small cooking fires. But in the fire's glow, the horror that surrounded them was overwhelming. Death and devastation from the Wilderness Campaign encircled them. Fragments of clothing, dead horses, shattered trees, and bodies were everywhere, for miles in each direction. The fires were quickly extinguished.

By dawn, Grant and his Union troops arrived, only to find out that the Confederates had arrived first. The rebels dug in and were able to repel several attempts by the North to take the crossroads. Unwilling to retreat, General Grant gave the order to reposition and prepare to attack at night fall. Several of the Union generals prior to Grant would have left the battlefield, but this was the final push by the Union troops. End was near, he could feel it.

Confederates were positioned behind an impressive line of defense. An earthen wall, with sharpened stakes and felled trees sticking out maliciously, snaked through the woods. This completely separated the Union soldiers from the crossroads and Richmond, Virginia, beyond. In the center of the giant rampart was a one miles long bulge that was called the Mule Shoe Salient. Grant carefully surveyed what lay in front of him. There had to be weak spot. All he had to do was find it!

As expected, the rebels dug in; and as darkness fell, more and more men were fed into the ensuing battle. It was like Wilderness all over again. Continuous musket and cannon fire cut a standing tree line in half. The dead and dying where moved to the back of each unit's line, keeping the battlefield providing room for the deadly assault to continue. In the chaos, bodies were stacked, the living and dead together in one morbid heap.

Grant was unable to out maneuver General Lee, but he would outgun him, hammer away at his defense until the Confederate troop split in two.

And then the rain began.

The rain collected in the rebel trenches, threatening to drown the injured and sweep away the living. The Confederates scrambled to relocate their ammunition.

General Grant used this to his advantage. As the Confederate troops stopped momentarily to protect their precious gunpowder, Grant gave the order. Twelve Union regiments quietly packed through the damp woods and charged the center of the defensive line, the Mule Shoe Salient.

The attack was impressive. Quick and deadly. Then just as quickly, the Northern troops pulled back to the safety of the woods again and began to prepare for the next onslaught.

The rain continued, turning the Virginia soil red with watered down blood.

Then on May the 12 at dawn, twenty thousand Union soldiers prepared to attack one more time. In the early dawn, using the morning mist as cover, the rebels were again caught unaware. The Union troops swarmed across the ramparts and successfully broke the Confederate line in two. Northern troops killed and captured thousands of rebels. Lee had just repositioned twenty-two cannons from this spot, completely misjudging Grant's next move.

The Confederates held their line for most of the day. Thousands of soldiers trudging through mud and blood as the rain continued relentlessly. The roar of the cannons, the muskets, and the men screaming, groaning, and even praying filled the air.

Everywhere was evidence that death was at work.

The battle raged on for over twenty hours until the sun shone its timid head. Grant was unable to pry Lee out of his earthen works, so the Union forces maneuvered eastward. Spotsylvania was a field of death.

Mud and corpses littered the valley. And there was no clear victory.

Hans Nilsson felt victorious. God had seen fit to see him through this hell.

Friend or Foe?

"MARY JANE! MARY Jane!" Nettie had to shake Mary Jane awake. She had fallen into a surprisingly deep slumber. Emotional exhaustion, no doubt.

"Mary Jane!" Nettie was frantic.

"Baby Hans, listen to him breathe!" There was panic in Nettie's voice, and tears were streaming down her face. The baby's breath was shallow and slow. He was dying, and Mary Jane knew it.

Mary Jane stood and took the baby from Nettie. She held him close to her chest and put her lips on his forehead. He was cold and clammy. Time was running out. They had to go now! The nearest neighbor was Mr. and Mrs. Parson. It took only over an hour to get to their farm by horse. Walking would take longer, but what choice did she have. None of the neighbors had come to check on the Nilsson children since Papa had left with the Union soldiers. They were all no doubt struggling to make an existence here as well. But Mrs.

Parson would know what to do, and she would be able to help this dying infant in her arms.

Mary Jane hastily climbed up the five steps and pushed open the solid cellar door. It flew open and landed on the floor with a thud. The house was warm, stiffening so. She walked to the back door and quickly grabbed the leather handle, then flung it open.

Tears instantly sprang to her eyes as she took in the panoramic view of the garden area. They were not alone. The cabin was surrounded.

Indians, everywhere. Three men were standing near the dry creek bed. Women sat in the dirt and on the porch. Several young men moved around the barn, and a few more stood looking down on the graves of Mama and Charlie. They were too late to escape. All eyes were upon her as she stood in the doorway, cradling the dying baby. Mary Jane could not move. She could not breathe. She was too late. She had failed to protect them.

Mary Jane sank to her knees, clutching Baby Hans to her chest. She felt frail, exhausted, beaten. She had let her family down. She had let Papa down. The tears began to flow freely, quietly streamed down her face where they disappeared into the collar of her soiled, calico dress.

The Indian who had come to the cabin only a few hours before strode up from the creek bed. His red handprinted face still clearly visible across the yard. With a deer slung over his right shoulder, he seemed even larger now. With only a few long, strong strides,

⇝ MARY JANE ⇜

he cleared the garden area and approached the back porch were he deposited his cargo.

"*Kino waiba.*" He had said these words to her earlier. Mary Jane, of course, still did not understand them. Her eyes met his and openly wept.

The man looked to a woman to his left and quietly spoke. The Indian woman slowly stood and walked toward Mary Jane, then reached her hands out for the baby. Mary Jane had no choice. She handed him over.

A defeated whimper escaped her mouth. Baby Hans made not a sound in his weakened state. The woman sat again, this time cradling the baby to her breast. She moved the hide skin dress to the side and began to nurse the starving infant.

The woman cradling her baby brother looked at Mary Jane with eyes warm as the summer grass, and repeated the Indian man's words. "*Kino waiba.*" All will be alright.

Her voice was calm and comforting.

In an instant, Mary Jane understood.

These people were not here to hurt her family.

They were here to save them.

Appomattox

"IT IS WITH pain that I announce to your Excellency the surrender of the Army of North Virginia," wrote General Robert E. Lee in his final report to the Confederate President, Jefferson Davis.

It was the afternoon of Sunday, April 9, 1865. After four long and bloody years the Civil War was officially over. General Lee anxiously waited at the Appomattox Court house in Virginia. General Grant's final campaign, assisted by the unrelenting devastation that swept through the south as Sherman and his armies marched to the sea, was more than the rebels could withstand.

The formalities of the surrender would take place in the front parlor of the two story white clap board building. This was the home of Wilmer McLean and was used as the community's courthouse only because of its size and accommodating rooms. Ironically, Wilmer McLean and his family had moved south to Appomattox after the first battle of the Civil War, Bull

Run. It began in his back field. The great war started in Wilmer McLean's back yard and ended in his front parlor.

General Lee was accompanied by his military secretary, Colonel Charles Marshal. Both were dressed in full uniform, out of a sense of etiquette. General Lee was always the gentlemen. After a forced retreat from the latest battle, both men had been required to retreat leaving behind their luggage and other personal belongings. The uniforms they wore today were the same ones they had been wearing on the battlefield when the surrender was agreed upon. General Robert E. Lee sat patiently with his hands clasped in his lap. He silently brushed away dust from his coat sleeve. His calm demeanor hid the conflict he must have been feeling.

General Grant arrived with a small battalion. As he strode up the steps, the Union general was flanked by eight of his most trusted officers. They were all smartly dressed in full campaign dress, freshly bathed and laundered.

The terms of surrender were simple. Grant demanded rolls and rosters of all Confederate soldiers. Each man was to turn in his weapon, give up his patrol, and swear to not take up arms against the United States Government again. With this came a pardon, and United States citizenship would be reinstated.

In addition, General Grant had asked for all cavalrymen to turn over their horses. General Lee informed Grant that the Confederate cavalrymen, and artillerymen as well, owned their own horses. They were personal property, not commissioned by the Confederate Army. He asked they be allowed to keep their mounts.

"I take it that most of the men in the ranks are small farmers," Grant began.

"Yes," Lee stated, ready to argue the case further.

That would not, however, be necessary.

Grant continued to think aloud. "As the country has been raided by two armies, it is doubtful whether they will be able to put in a crop to carry themselves and their families through the next winter without aid of these horses…Yes." The general nodded. "They shall keep their mounts," Grant said as he looked over his shoulder to his secretary who was carefully listening to everything as he prepared the necessary documents for the surrender.

It was more than a gesture of generosity. Grant knew that this day marked the first day of healing for the nation. Brother would have to forgive brother. Neighbor would have to learn to trust neighbor again. And it would start here with these two powerful military leaders.

"This will have the best possible effect upon the men," General Lee stated in appreciation. "It will be very gratifying and will do much toward conciliating our people."

A further gesture of generosity and healing was extended in the form of twenty-five thousand food rations. These were to be sent immediately to the camps, where the confederates were hardest hit and no doubt starving.

General Lee then gave his final address: After four years of arduous service marked by renowned courage… for your consistency and devotion to your country…I bid you all an affectionate farewell." It was signed R. E. Lee.

As General Lee left the Appomattox Court House, Union cavalrymen dressed in their blue uniforms dismounted from their horses and saluted the mastermind that had led the Confederate forces for four years. General Lee had graduated from West Point at the top of class. He was a brilliant tactician and a true leader of men. President Abraham Lincoln had even tried to recruit him to lead the Union forces. But Robert E. Lee's heart was Southern, through and through. And for that, he had lost everything.

When the first wounded Union soldiers arrived on the steps of the White House after the First Bull Run, Lincoln was ill prepared. The city of Washington had no place to bury so many dead. It had been suggested to take them across the Potomac River and bury them at General Lee's plantation. And so it was.

The first casualties of the Civil War were buried in Mrs. Lee's rose garden. In front of their beloved plantation house—Arlington House. Thousands more would follow. Turning the Lee Plantation into America's largest cemetery, later to be known as Arlington Cemetery.

The cost of the war weighed heavy on all Americans. With over six hundred thousand dead, thousands more wounded and missing, how could we ever heal? How could we ever rebuild our nation? Rebuild our lives?

The first step was to go home.

The Village

THE NILSSON CHILDREN were well rested and fed. They had their strength and color back in their cheeks. Mary Jane was constantly amazed at how easy and comfortable it was to be with the People. They were kind, gentle, and full of laughter. They were Chippewa, Ojibwa, Indian. But to her, they were her saviors.

It was apparent after spending only a few days with the People, that the man, who wore a red hand painted across his mouth and chin, was a man of importance in the tribe. A shaman, a medicine man. The people looked to him for guidance and answers. He was often thoughtful and quiet. Mary Jane was still a bit afraid of him but much less so than earlier. The boys, however, thought he was amazing and were usually trailing behind him like hungry quail. His people called him Nooka, Tender Bear.

The people spoke a language that was unfamiliar to the children. However, several hand gestures were regularly used. This combined with the fact that quite a few of the Indians spoke a mixture of French and even a little English made communication slow and tedious but accessible. Every day Alfred, Eric, George, and Isaar bragged to Mary Jane about what they had learned today. The Chippewa word for this, the Chippewa word for that.

"Mary Jane, you are an *ikwaywug*, a woman," Eric would state with pride.

"Mary Jane, this is my *ozid*, my foot!" Isaar happily exclaimed.

"Mary Jane, we are *nini*, men!" She heard this more than once, always with pride.

"Mary Jane, we are *neezhodays*, twins!" George added.

"Mary Jane, we are *giwisayininiwug*, hunters," called another.

Mary Jane had a more descriptive word in her mind as to what these boys were, but she doubted it could easily be translated into Ojibwa.

Days turned to weeks, weeks to months. It was obvious the People were ready to move on now. Mary Jane feared they would leave them just as she had begun to feel safe again.

She had slept through the night for the first time since Papa left. She so appreciated the companionship of these gentle, caring people. She did not want them to go. She dreaded the day they would.

The following morning, when the Indians packed up to leave, the Nilsson children lined up along the cabins back porch, and tears fell freely. The woman who had been taking care of and feeding Baby Hans stood in front of Mary Jane and looked her in the eyes.

Mary Jane swallowed hard. It would be difficult to say good-bye to this kind woman. A woman who so freely gave so much of herself to a child that was not her own, not even the same color as her own. These people were nothing like the horror stories she had been told.

The friendly face smiled, and then she spoke with her voice as well as her hands.

First, she pointed to Mary Jane and waved her hand along the line of Nilsson children, and then she laid her hands across her own chest. "*Peonagowink. Kino waiba.*"

This time, it was her voice that washed over the children. Mary Jane had heard these words before, the first words the shaman Nooka, Tender Bear, had said to her when he entered the cabin that frightful day so many weeks ago.

"*Peonagowink. Kino waiba.*" Come with me. All will be all right.

They were not going to leave the children behind. They were going to take them with them. With only a slight hesitation at leaving Papa's cabin, the children followed their new friends past the wild rose bush and over the creek bed into the wilderness beyond.

They walked north for days, but the Nilsson children did not complain. There was plenty of rests, time to swim, and always enough food to eat. In the evening, the women set up the wigwams while the men took the boys hunting. After the sunset, they gathered around a warm fire, comfortable and full. The dwellings were full of chatter and laughter. The children were being cuddled and patted, and with full bellies, they fell asleep with their head in a loving lap.

The People were patient and kind as they tended and taught the Nilsson children. They taught them about the land, the trees, and the water. They taught them to read trails and watch for signs of game. They taught them their language, one word at a time. Within a very short time, the children were acting and thinking like their new friends.

"What do I call you?" Mary Jane had asked the young woman who had saved Baby Hans and cared for them all so lovingly.

"*Ikway?*" she replied as she brushed the tangles from Mary Jane's hair with a bone comb.

"Woman?" Mary Jane gasped. "No! That would never do. You are so much more than just a woman to me!" she continued, struggling with the translation.

The Chippewa word for *Mama* and *Papa* were a unique personal name between a parent and a child. But there was one special word, *nokomis*. Grandmother. It was a word demonstrating love and respect for a wise woman who shared much of herself with you.

"May I call you Nokomis?" Mary Jane asked timidly.

There were no words in answer to this question, just a tight bear hug and a face covered with sweet, tender kisses. Mary Jane guessed *Nokomis* approved of her new name.

The Chippewa village constituted of hundreds of oval-shaped wooden lodges. Wigwams. Each lodge was neatly arranged around the banks of the Red Lake in northern Minnesota. The wigwams were built with a sturdy frame made of flexible tamarack or white ash saplings. Post ends were buried several inches into the earth, bent and tied with bark strips. Other saplings were then woven through to produce the domed structure of this semi-permanent dwelling. The wigwam was then covered with cedar bark. Tightly woven rush mats covered the dirt floors. Inside, along the sides of the wigwam were piles of skins and furs. Thick buffalo fur bedding was neatly arranged ready to offer comfort and warmth for the sleepy.

A central fire pit was surrounded by blackened stones. Here smoke lazily curled out of the hole in the roof. A copper pot hung over the fire heavy with aroma of elk meat stewing.

Each wigwam faced east, so at every exit, you would welcome the new day.

Vegetable gardens were planted and neatly tended. The people referred to their garden as the Three Sisters. Neatly spaced mounds held corn stalks that were already taller than Mary Jane's head. The cornstalks served as the pole for the beans to cling to. The bean added much-needed nitrogen to the hungry soil. Then entwining both plants were the lush green leaves and stems of squash, providing ground cover and shade for the roots of the other two crops. Theses were the three sisters, living in harmony, corn, beans, and squash.

Seeing the squash plants caused a pang to Mary Jane's chest, as she remembered her little brother Charlie. Charlie hated squash. That was a day Mary Jane would not soon forget.

Across a well-worn path, happy faces of sunflowers lifted their chins to the sky. The people had also planted pumpkins, gourds, artichokes, and ground cherries. Surrounding it all were several well tended tobacco plants. The tobacco was a very important crop to the People. Tobacco was used for ceremonial offerings, smoked in the sacred red stone pipes. It was, as were the other crops, considered gifts from the creator.

These crops supplemented the food gathered in the woods, wild rice, camas roots, wild onions, nuts and berries, and of course, what was hunted by the men. Elk, deer, bear, fowl, and fish were staples. Red Lake provided it all. Hunting parties would regularly move as far east as Lake Superior and hunt north into Canada, but they always returned home to Red Lake, where the wild rice grew. It was this territory that spoke to their spirits—it was this land they called home. They had been forced to leave, thanks to yet another treaty, and they did as they were instructed. However, when they followed the game, it led them right back home. The creator wanted them here, so here they would stay as long as the whites were busy with their Civil War. As long as they could live undetected. Scouts were sent out in order to protect the village. It was these eyes that had witnessed with great sadness what was unfolding on the Nilsson farm.

Scouts had apparently been interested in the Nilsson farm for a while. They too had seen the giant dust cloud approach the farm, the dust cloud that was in fact the Union soldiers arriving to take Papa away. The scouts had witnessed the drought and the locusts, and they knew about the drowning death of little Charlie. Mary Jane had long since learned it was a hunting party that had returned to their village with the story of little Charlie's death. Nooka (Tender Bear) himself had ridden out to see the pale-faced children struggling to survive. That was yet another day Mary Jane would never forget.

According to Chippewa tradition, in order for a guest to be welcomed into the home or into the tribal clan, it has to be approved by the women of the tribe. The women own the wigwam; therefore, they have the ultimate say as to who is welcome and who is not.

Mary Jane would never learn who had made the decision to welcome her and her brothers and sisters. But she would be eternally grateful. The shaman Tender Bear was then sent to find out how many children there were. He was perplexed when the fiery girl tried to beat him off with a frying pan. Again, the women of the Red Lake Clan took charge and came directly to the cabin to retrieve the children. Now they were an extended part of this large loving family.

They had daily chores of gathering wood, drying meat, tending the children, and preparing clothing and meals. The boys hunted and fished daily as well as continued with the lessons of tracking, scouting, and protecting the village. It was a happy life, full of companionship and laughter.

Mary Jane and the children shared the wigwam with Nokomis, Grandmother. Nokomis was too young to be a grandmother. She was a young mother and had two small boys of her own, just babies. They all shared a home with her husband, Rolling Thunder. This wigwam had a stream of important visitors. The shaman Nooka came to visit regularly. As did Baswenaazhi, Chief Crane. Some day, Rolling Thunder would be a chief in the Red Lake Clan. Tonight, they all sat around the central fire. They ate delicious stew from wooden bowls. Nokomis had made a flat bread to soak up the juices. The children were quietly slurping up the delectable meal, comfortable with their surroundings.

Then Chief Crane spoke. "You are a welcome sight in this village," he began. "Are you happy here?" He glanced around the fire.

The children nodded their heads, very satisfied with everything this night.

"And you, Mary Jane?" he asked. "Are you happy to be with the People?"

Mary Jane swallowed a chunk of meat, then thought for a moment before she replied.

"Yes. I am happy and very grateful for what you and the People have done for my brothers and sisters." Her eyes found the soft brown eyes of Grandmother. They filled with tears as she looked at the women she had rapidly grown to love. Salty tears spilled down her cheeks.

Chief Crane was a strong and well-respected leader of his people and had been for many moons. He knew instinctively that this young woman, now one of his people, had more to say. He remained quiet. Patient. Listening.

Mary Jane was thankful for the moment to collect herself before she continued. Wiping the tears from her face, she again turned her attention to the chief. She took a deep cleansing breath before she continued.

"I worry for my father. When he returns from war, how will he find us? I worry that he will be disappointed that I left the cabin, the garden, and my mama and Charlie." Her voice caught with this final word.

This was something felt strongly by the People as well. Their land was sacred to them because this is where their loved ones were buried. This concern had already crossed the mind of Chief Crane. He addressed her questions with a legend. Oral traditions passed down around the hearth fires was the way in which the People taught their children. It taught them about their past and offered guidance for their future.

"Wenebojo was the first Chippewa, the first Ojibwa. He was very brave and had defeated evil many times," he began.

All listened eagerly and attentively.

His voice continued, strong and smooth like molasses dripping from the trees. "One day, Wenebojo was walking along by the edge of the lake. He saw some high bush cranberries lying in the shallow water. He stuck his hand in the water and tried to fish them out, but he couldn't reach them. He tried over and over again to get those cranberries. Finally, he gave up trying to stick his hand in the water, and instead, he tried to grab them with his mouth by sticking his head under the water. That did not work either. So he dove into the water. But the water was so shallow that little rocks on the bottom cut his face. He jumped out of the water and lay down on his back on the shore, cradling his hurt face in his hands. When he finally opened his eyes, he noticed there were the berries hanging directly above him! The berries were in the trees, not in the water. He had only seen their reflection." With that, he paused and looked directly into Mary Jane's green eyes. "You see, everything in not always what it appears," he said, looking directly into her young, green eyes. "Be patient and problems tend to work themselves out. Scouts will continue to watch. And when your father comes home, they will alert us," Crane said softly.

Then he reached for his wooden bowl to enjoy more stew. He would not get to eat much as Mary Jane emotionally threw her arms around his neck.

The Sultana

WITH LEE'S SURRENDER at Appomattox, the fate of the Confederacy was sealed. But news traveled slowly across the nation. On April 26, General Johnston surrendered to Sherman in North Carolina. And by the end of May, the scattered forces of the confederation had almost all laid down their arms. General Stan Waite was the last to surrender. So on June 23, 1865, the war was finally over.

Washington, DC, was busy rebuilding. President Lincoln was pushing for his Freedman's Bureau to pass Congress. The Freedman's Bureau would offer all newly freed blacks assistance to find food, clothing, shelter, schools, and more importantly, work. Every one knew this was only Lincoln's first step. Next, he would be pushing for all black men to be citizens and have the right to vote.

Money was almost nonexistent. Confederate money was useless paper, mostly used in outhouses across the

South. Union funds were slow to reach soldiers below the Mason-Dixon Line. Transportation home for soldiers was also nonexistent. Hans Nilsson was deep in the South, hundreds of miles from his home and children in Minnesota. This territory was unlike anything he had seen. It was war ravaged. Towns and cities devastated, nothing but rubble. The people were in still in shock and not able to offer a stranded soldier assistance, even if they had wanted to.

Hans knew his best chance to get home was to follow the Mississippi River north. He had heard of a steam wheeler that was taking on Union soldiers, free of charge. The name of this ship was the *Sultana*.

The *Sultana*. That was his goal. Getting on board that river boat, heading north, heading home.

The rest of the nation, however, was focused on another matter. Just six days after the surrender at Appomattox, the unthinkable occurred. An actor and Confederate sympathizer named John Wilkes Booth shot and killed the president. The nation was in shock. Even people who despised President Lincoln mourned his loss. He was every American's best chance at healing the nation quickly.

On Good Friday, April 14, 1865, Booth made it into the Presidential Box at Ford's Theater. The President and his wife were joined by friends, Major Henry Rathbone and his fiancée, Clara Harris, for a well-deserved evening off. They were enjoying a stage performance of the comedy, *Our American Cousin*. Booth used his Philadelphia Derringer pistol to shoot Lincoln in the back of the head before jumping to the stage below. Here he faced the stunned audience and cried, "*Sic Semper Tyrannis!*" It was Latin for "Thus ever to tyrants."

Mary Lincoln's and Clara Harris's screams joined Rathbone's cries of "Stop that man!" This alerted the audience that this was not part of the stage presentation. But Booth had made it successfully out of the theater where a saddled horse awaited him to aid his escape from the city.

Three doctors and a few soldiers who had been in the audience carried the president out the front doors of the theater. Across the street, a man named Henry Safford held a lantern and called out to them urgently.

"Bring him in here! Bring him in here!"

The men carried the president into the Petersen Boarding House. They took him to the first-floor bedroom and laid him diagonally on the bed, and the vigil began. Dr. Robert Stone, who was the president's personal physician, was sent for, as well as the Lincoln's eldest son Robert. Nothing could be done. The bullet had lodged itself directly behind the president's right eye. In the early morning hours, the crowd around his bed knelt in prayer. And at 7:22 a.m. on April 15, 1865, he took his last raspy breath.

"Now he belongs to the ages," whispered Secretary Stanton with a heavy heart.

The nation was gripped with the dramatic hunt for Booth, the largest manhunt in American history. The Lincoln family began to plan the president's funeral, which would be one for the record books.

Hans listened to others as they read from local newspapers. His spoken English was strong, but reading it was another story. His heart ached for the Lincoln family and now for a nation that would struggle to rebuild under the leadership of their new president, Andrew Johnson. But his mind was on his own family. His goal was to get home to his children.

The SS *Sultana* was a Mississippi River steam paddle wheeler. With Captain J. C. Mason at the helm, this steamboat would take any soldier north. Hans arrived at the docks of Vicksburg, Mississippi, with about two thousand other Union soldiers. Many had recently been released from the Confederate prison camp, Andersonville. Hundreds of these men were nothing but walking skeletons, evidence that the severely harsh conditions in these camps were not exaggerated.

Over two thousand four hundred passengers were packed into every available berth. The overflow was so severe that the decks were completely full. Standing room only. But the mood was jovial—they were going home, all of them. Home!

After a small patch repair was made to one of her four boilers, fuel coal was loaded and the whistle blew. The *Sultana* chugged against the current, heading north up the Mississippi River.

Hans had to sleep standing up, leaning against the ships railing. He did not mind. Each day brought him one day closer to Minnesota and his children. It had been almost a year and a half since he had seen their faces. But he had promised to return. He smiled, relieved that this was a promise he was able to keep. He inhaled deeply; the air was moist, clean, and refreshing. Tears leaked from the corners of his eyes, tears of liberation.

This evening, they were nine miles north of Memphis Tennessee. It was April, 27, 1865. In the early morning hour of 2:00 a.m., there was a horrific explosion in the boiler room. It rocked the overcrowded ship, spilling several passengers from the deck into the icy water of the Mississippi River. A second explosion destroyed a large portion of the ship and set the wooden barge on fire. Hot coals scattered by the explosions soon turned the *Sultana* into a floating inferno.

Passengers who survived the initial explosions had to risk their lives in the icy spring runoff of the Mississippi River or burn to death. Hundreds fled the sweeping fire and steam eruptions for the black churning waters.

The south bound steamer the *Bostonia II* will be the first ship to arrive on the scene of the disaster. It was 3:00 a.m. Immediately, they began to pluck survivors from the water. By sunrise, other ships had joined the rescue effort, including the steamer *Arkansas*, the *Jenny Lind*, the *Essex*, and the Navy gunboat, the USS *Tyler*. Soon, it was obvious; it was no longer a rescue mission but a recovery effort. Bodies were everywhere. They floated in the river, laid on the banks, even hung in the trees. Many died of drowning or hypothermia. Victims' bodies will be discovered down river for months to come, some as far south as Vicksburg.

The remains of the *Sultana* drifted to the western bank and sank just after dawn near the little settlement of Mound City, Arkansas.

Over five hundred survivors, suffering from appalling burns, were taken to several Memphis Hospitals. Less than half of them will survive medical treatments. Memphis will also be the location the dead would be buried. The death toll was staggering. An estimated one thousand eight hundred of the two thousand four hundred passengers and crew were killed, including Captain Mason.

The official cause of the *Sultana* disaster will be a mystery for many years. A St. Louis resident and Southern conspirator, Robert Louden, will claim responsibility. Louden claims he built several "coal bombs" that were loaded onto the *Sultana* in Vicksburg. The coal bombs had the appearance of an ordinary chunk of coal but were, in actuality, an iron ball with a cored center, full of gunpowder.

The Sultana Disaster is considered the worst US maritime disaster in American history and may very well be the first major terrorist attack as well. Hans Nilsson was one of the lucky ones. He found himself on the western bank of the Mississippi River. Here, he briefly rested before he continued on his voyage home.

Home

~~~~~~~~~~∞~~~~~~~~~~

AFTER TWO LONG years, Hans Nilsson finally recognized the land on which he walked. This was Minnesota. He was only miles away from the town of Brainerd, and north of that was his small wooden cabin with the rock cellar and fireplace that he and his family had built.

He could picture the bubbling creek he himself had named Little Creek. He could picture the wild rose bush covered with heavenly scented white blossoms that draped over his beloved Bertha's grave. He knew every beam in the barn, every log in the cabin—every smile on the faces that would greet him. How much had they grown? Would they recognize him? He wondered for the thousandth time.

His heartbeat increased with his pace.

If he kept this pace, he could be home by dusk.

The town seemed smaller, dirtier. Hans wasted no time. Years of training had built in him the timing required of a smart man's march. He kept the pace. As the sun dipped behind the hills, he came to the final bend in the dirt road. Within moments, he would view the homestead.

His eyes were not prepared for what greeted him.

The roof had caved in, and the barn was nothing but rubble. The stone fireplace stood tall and proud, but the rest of the homestead was crumbling from neglect around it. The garden area was nothing but weeds and crab grass. And under the blooming wild rose bush was not one grave, but two.

There were no children running out to greet him. No laughter, no hugs. No little arms wrapping around his tired, lonely neck. Where were his children? It had been almost two years. What had happened to his family? A heavy weight swept through his chest, making it impossible to breathe. Again, he chided himself for thinking that coming to America was a good idea for them. How wrong he had been.

He lay on the back porch and cried himself to sleep.

Hans Nilsson had lost track of time. He had no recollection as to how many days he sat on that porch, or was it merely hours? When the Indian brave walked over the creek and to the porch, he did not even blink. Perhaps this would be the end of his suffering.

The man simply looked down at him, and then quietly, he spoke. "*Boozhoo,*" The brave said, gesturing with his hands as well. Greetings.

Hans made no reply.

"*Aanii.*" Hello. Again, Hans made no attempt of replying.

Just end my life here and now, he silently prayed.

"*Beindigain OdYnhwing.*" Come, come with me to the village.

Hans did not understand a word this Indian warrior was saying. But he followed him obediently. Walking steps behind the young man. The Indians strides were long and strong. The step of a young man with a purpose. Hans shuffled his feet, dragging them enough to stir up a dust cloud behind him. He had no purpose.

They walked for days. Past countless rivers and lakes. Thick forests of pine and deciduous trees surrounded them. The beauty of the scenery held no pleasure for Hans. He looked through unseeing eyes as he meandered behind the scout. The Indian stopped and built a fire. He offered Hans the hind leg of a wild jackrabbit. Hans gnawed on the leg bone unconsciously. He slept and arose without fuss as the sun rose above the hills. They continued on for another day without saying a word. Hans made no eye contact, so he could not see the sadness in his companion's face.

As the sun dressed in it's evening pink attire on the fifth day, Hans became alert for the first time of this unique journey. They stood atop a sloping hill. Below them spread out along the banks of a giant and very beautiful lake, Red Lake was a sprawling Indian village. Wigwams were neatly organized along the banks of the turquoise water. Torches had been lit along the shore. Campfires and cooking fires shone brightly within neatly stacked stones. Hides hung over drying racks. Horses grazed in the meadow, and children scampered and played nearby. Their laughter rang out like a song in the early evening.

Perhaps it was the sound of innocent laughter that brought Hans out of his trance. He sucked in his breath as he took in the panoramic view of a people, entire families, untouched by the horrors he had recently experienced.

Women were working, men were preparing for nightfall, and children were running, playing, and talking. Gradually, the fog lifted from his mind. His guide instinctively knew Hans needed a moment to collect his thoughts and graciously allowed it. He stood next to Hans in strong and silent vigilance.

Hans Nilsson squinted his eyes. He looked to his guide, and upon a shrug of his shoulder and his outstretched hand, he allowed his gaze to follow.

What was it he was supposed to see?

Why had this man brought him here?

He took a closer look at the youth scampering between the field and the torch lit lake bed. The children were all dressed in buckskins, hair flying behind them, wild and free. The language they spoke was foreign to his ears, but the laughter was universal. The sound made tears sting his eyes. He wiped them away with the back of his dirty hand.

And then he saw them.

Their faces were tanned with a healthy glow. Their clothing was native. They were dressed in hides. But the hair coloring and yes, the eyes he remembered. Well.

There was one, and another, another, and yet another one there.

There, laughing and *living* in this dream-like setting were his children.

Mary Jane heard the talking outside the dwellings. The people were excited. The guide had returned. She quickly ducked her head as she excited the wigwam, Grandmother just a few steps behind her. She held her hand up shading her eyes as she scanned the horizon. Then she saw him.

"It's Papa," she breathlessly whispered. Tears freely ran down both checks as years of worry ebbed away. "He's home!"

Silently, Grandmother slipped her hand into Mary Jane's and squeezed it lovingly.

"Now you are all home," she said to Mary Jane.

Yes, they were.

Home.

Epilogue

THE NILSSON FAMILY had its share of tragedies, but they also had many blessings. They were reunited. Alive and well because a group of people were able and willing to look past war, hate, and prejudice.

The Chippewa people shared only *zahgidiwin*, love.

Mary Jane felt it all around her. It was a father's love and desire for a better life for his family that brought the Nilssons to America. It was love and willpower to keep a promise that brought Hans Nilsson home from the brutality of the Civil War. It was love that gave Mary Jane and her siblings the strength to continue. And it was love for life that brought the People to the Nilssons' cabin door.

Love and compassion—the truest test of the human spirit.

The reunited Nilssons spent the majority of their lives living in close proximity to their family, the Red Lake Band of the Chippewa Indians. The Chippewa

Tribe was successful in resisting several relocation efforts north. After the Civil War, it was discovered that a land survey error had misplaced the border between the United States and Canada. With the border location adjustment, The Old Crossing Treaty of 1863 stipulated that land around the Red Lake area belonged to the Chippewa People. It is today, the largest Native American reservation in the state of Minnesota. The reservation covers over one thousand two hundred square miles with the Red Lake as its heart.

Mary Jane and Nettie will become teachers. Their first class was a room full of eager Chippewa children wanting to learn to read and write English. Several of the Nilsson children will marry and become farmers in northern Minnesota. They will live only miles from Red Lake as will their children and their children's children.

Hans's dream had come true. America did provide a better life for his family.

Hans Nilsson never remarried but found much joy in watching his children grow up and find true love of their own. He died at the age of sixty-four. He is buried in Northern Minnesota where the wild roses grow.

Mary Jane would meet and marry John Wilhelm Anderson. They had a small but successful farm outside of Brainerd, Minnesota, just south of Red Lake. Here they raised their children to love the land and respect all. As the years passed and Mary Jane's grown children set off to make they own lives, she marveled at the lessons they took with them.

Mary Jane's oldest daughter, Vivian, became a pioneer teacher in the new state of Minnesota. Another daughter, Surrie, would marry and eventually work for the US government in Washington, DC. Her sons, George and Aleck, remained at home and helped with the family farm until adventure called them north to Alberta, Canada. Young Mary, seemingly Mary Jane's last child, married John Anderson (Uncle Johnny) and moved to Oakland California where she became a nurse.

Years passed, and Mary Jane found herself pregnant for the sixth time. A change-of-life baby, unexpected but treasured. This sixth child is my grandmother, Mabel.

Mary Jane followed her daughter Mary, to Oakland, California, in her later years. She brought with her young Mabel. Mabel would marry and raise her own family in California.

Mary Jane lived to be 101 years old.

She shared her story and her wisdom lovingly.

She is buried in the Pioneer Cemetery in Prattville, California.

We visit her often. Because she was a much beloved *nokomis*, grandmother.

※ Anne Marie Fritz ※

He who loves the haunts of Nature,
Love the sunshine of the meadow,
Love the shadow of the forest,
Love the wind among the branches,
And the rain-shower and the snowstorm,
And the rushing of great rivers
Through their palisades of pine-trees,
And the thunder in the mountains,
Whose innumerable echoes
Flap like eagles in their iris,
Listen to these wild traditions,
To this Song of Hiawatha!

By the shores of Gitche Gumee,
By the shining Big-Sea-Water,
Stood the wigwam of Nokomis,
Daughter of the Moon, Nokomis.
Dark behind it rose the forest,
Rose the black and gloomy pine-trees,
Rose the firs with cones upon them;
Bright before it beat the water,
Beat the clear and sunny water,
Beat the shining Big-Sea-Water.

—Henry Wadsworth Longfellow
"The Song of Hiawatha"

This is a poem written to honor the Chippewa Indians. The end of one story, but the beginning of many more!